AGENT CODY BANKS 2: DESTINATION LONDON

Junior Novelization
Adapted by Michael Anthony Steele

Screenplay by
Don Rhymer

Story by
Harald Zwart & Dylan Sellers
and Don Rhymer

Based on the Characters Created by
Jeffrey Jurgensen

SCHOLASTIC INC.

New York Toronto London Auckland Sydney
Mexico City New Delhi Hong Kong Buenos Aires

ISBN 0-439-65125-5

12 11 10 9 8 7 6 5 4 3 4 5 6 7 8/0

Printed in the U.S.A.
First printing, March 2004

AGENT CODY BANKS 2: DESTINATION LONDON

1

DANGEROUSLY DANGLING

The sliding rope warmed his gloved hands as Agent Cody Banks rapelled down the side of the office building. When he reached the target floor, the young agent clamped down on his lifeline, halting his descent. Wind ruffled his dark-brown hair as he glanced toward the sidewalk several stories below. It was a long way down and he dangled from a tiny black rope. Cody wasn't scared though; he was elated. He was having the time of his life.

Getting back to the mission at hand, Cody placed his feet against the window, steadying himself. He reached into a pouch in his black jumpsuit and retrieved his PDA. This was no ordinary Personal Digital Assistant; this was CIA issue, the kind of high-tech equipment the Central Intelligence Agency issued their agents, even if their agents were teenagers like himself.

Cody opened a compartment, revealing a tiny round button. He removed the button and placed it onto the window in front of him. He tapped a switch and the PDA projected a 3-D holographic image of the room inside.

Cody was studying the map when he noticed a reflection in the window — one that wasn't his own. He ducked just as a black club swiped at his head. The blow missed him, smashing the window instead.

The young agent turned to see a man, also dangling from a rope and wielding a dark club. Holding on tightly to his rope, Cody turned and ran down the side of the building. When he reached the edge, he kicked off and used his momentum to whip around and swing toward his attacker. The man on the rope looked up just in time to see Cody's boots flying toward his face.

SMACK!

The man was knocked out cold, hanging limply from his rope.

Suddenly another dark figure dropped from above and wrapped his legs around Cody's neck. The young agent desperately swung at the attacker, but he couldn't land a solid blow. The man's thighs clamped tighter and Cody began to get light-headed. He had to find a way to escape before he lost consciousness.

Clutching desperately at his attacker's legs, Cody felt something in the man's pocket. He ripped open the Velcro flap and found cigarettes and a lighter. Throwing the cigarettes aside, he flicked open the lighter, and held the open flame under the man's butt. His enemy screamed as he released his grip. Cody reached over, pulled the buckle on the man's harness, and then kicked out of his reach. Cody swung on the rope as the man screamed, plummeting several stories to the ground below.

"When they said smoking was hazardous to your health," Cody smirked, "you should've listened."

Cody glanced up and saw that his rope had been rubbing against a shard of broken glass during the struggle. The frayed line was about to snap. He scrambled toward the window, but that only made the rope unravel faster. He knew he wouldn't make it. This mission was going to end very badly.

2

THE MOUSE AND THE CHEESE

As Cody desperately reached for the open window, someone tapped him on the shoulder.

"Hey, Cody!" said a voice behind him.

Cody turned to see a young boy standing just below him. He was standing where there should only be air. It was his friend and fellow agent, Ryan.

"I found this snake by the latrines," Ryan said, holding up a writhing green snake. "I'm going to put it in the girls' cabin. Want to come?"

Suddenly a loud buzzer sounded. Cody squinted as bright lights illuminated the dark city scene. People in lab coats stepped out from behind the office building, which wasn't a building at all. It was only a facade to simulate the tall structure. In fact, the entire city wasn't real. It was a high-tech simulation inside a large room. And Ryan wasn't standing in midair, but on top of a floor with a bird's-eye view of a city street projected onto it from underneath.

Cody was about to reply when his rope finally snapped and he dropped three feet to the ground. He landed next to one of his previous attackers. The man casually sat there reading a paperback novel.

"Oh . . . I guess you guys were busy, huh?" Ryan asked nervously. "And I pretty much just messed it up."

The ten-year-old boy looked quite out of place with his shorts and stained white T-shirt. Ryan looked around then slowly backed away from Cody and the building facade. After a couple of steps, he turned and darted toward the large exit door before he could get in trouble.

Cody stood and brushed himself off. He looked at the technicians gathered around. "Okay, wait a second," he said angrily. "The Central Intelligence Agency, the most sophisticated intelligence gathering operation in the world . . . but we don't have a 'Do Not Disturb' sign for the door?"

"Sorry Agent Banks," said a voice over the loudspeaker. "Let's run it again."

"Why?" Cody asked, looking up to the control room window. Several men in lab coats stared back at him. "I'm trying to break in exactly the way you taught me and every time something goes wrong."

"Maybe that's what *I'm* trying to teach you," said another voice.

Cody turned and saw Victor Diaz, one of his instructors. The dark-haired man stood there squeezing his little blue racquetball — something he always carried with him. He smirked and bounced it on the floor a couple of times.

"If you want to catch a mouse you don't tear out your walls," Diaz said, "you simply put out a little cheese." He spun around and marched toward the control room as the technicians prepared to rerun the simulation.

Cody just stood there, baffled. "What's that supposed to mean?"

A few hours and several simulations later, Cody stepped out of the training area and onto the porch of the old building. The weather-worn planks of the building paled in comparison to its ultra-modern interior. But that was the idea.

Cody gazed at the grounds of Kamp Woody. Ever since the CIA recruited him to be an agent, Cody had trained every summer at their secret facility. To most people, and parents especially, Kamp Woody seemed like just another summer camp. In reality, Kamp Woody trained young girls and boys to be CIA junior agents. Here they learned everything from how to utilize high-tech spy equipment to hand-to-hand combat.

A group of young boys ran up the steps to join Cody on the porch. Two of them were Cody's friends and fellow agents, Ryan and Bender.

"Cody, you've been on real missions," said Bender. With his buzz-cut head and large size, he didn't seem to be a "junior" anything. "Tell these guys, it's awesome, right?"

"Are you ever scared?" Ryan asked timidly. The young boy seemed frightened of everything but animals, insects, and most creepy-crawlers.

Bender gave Ryan a playful slap on the shoulder. "Dude, he's Cody Banks!"

Just then, four girls walked toward the group of boys. They did not look happy at all. Marisa, the oldest, held out Ryan's green snake.

She blew a strand of blond hair out of her face and pointed to Ryan. "Hand him over," she said. "He's ours."

Marisa placed the snake on the ground and it slithered into the bushes. Then she and the others snapped to various martial arts stances, getting ready for a fight. Cody had sparred with most of these girls in class and still had some of the bruises to prove it. They were proficient in many fighting styles and could attack with the stealth of ninjas.

Cody turned to Ryan. "You should have known these are not your typical camp girls."

Ryan stepped behind Cody for protection. "I knew I should've went to fat camp with my cousin."

All of a sudden, an alarm sounded.

"Attention all campers," cried a voice over the camp's speaker system. "Prepare the camp for Parents' Night. We have in-bound minivans on radar. This is not a drill. Repeat. This is not a drill!"

Forgetting their prey, the ninja girls ran back toward their cabin. The rest of the boys scattered in various directions as Cody ran back into the training simulator. Once inside, he lifted one of the floorboards and hit a secret switch. A false wall rose from the floor, covering the dark city skyline. Shelves full of T-shirts, candy, and postcards appeared from other secret panels. Soon the state-of-the-art simulation chamber was transformed into a run-of-the-mill camp store.

In another part of the camp, a black SUV skidded through a sharp turn on a driving course. Young campers quickly stepped in and directed the vehicle into an opening in the trees. Once they had covered the back of the SUV with branches, several campers on harmless go-karts emerged and raced around the track.

Near the lake, kids training with Japanese fighting sticks pressed buttons on their sticks causing flaps to shoot out of each end, transforming them to kayak paddles. Meanwhile kids exiting the lake with scuba gear, removed their gear and were handed inner tubes.

Once the transformation was complete, Cody changed out of his training jumpsuit and into shorts and a T-shirt. He strolled toward the parking lot looking for his parents.

"Hey, Mom!" shouted Cody as he saw his approaching family. His mom and dad gazed at the camp, while Cody's little brother, Alex, clumsily hid something in his pocket.

"Dad, you look great," Cody said, shaking his father's hand. "You made good time. Did you take the '64' to the bypass, or straight down the '15'?"

His dad seemed dumbfounded by such a mature question coming from his teenage son. "Uh, the bypass," he replied.

"Wise choice," Cody commented. He turned to his brother. "Alex, little man, you've certainly . . ." Cody broke off his compliment when he glanced into his brother's pocket. "Is that my Gameboy?"

Alex looked a bit worried. "Uh, I don't know, I found it in . . ."

"It's okay," Cody interrupted. "You can have it. Enjoy."

While Alex looked at Cody with disbelief, Cody placed his arms around his parents' shoulders. He ushered them toward the dining hall.

"We have some time before the bonfire, can I get you guys something to drink?" asked Cody.

Cody's parents were speechless. It seemed as if their oldest son had matured greatly during his stay at summer camp.

3

BETRAYAL

That night, Cody lay in his bunk and stared at the ceiling. Most of the kids in his cabin were already asleep. Bender snored and drooled on his pillow, while Ryan picked up a passing spider and held it close as if it were a teddy bear. Cody simply thought of his family's visit.

They couldn't believe how maturely he behaved. He didn't threaten to kill his brother once and he even refused to take money from his mom. He had told them that he wasn't a kid anymore so he wasn't going to act like one. What he *hadn't* told them was that he was really a famous secret agent who loved all the adventure and excitement that came with it. He had plenty of new responsibilities now and didn't have time for being a kid.

Suddenly, as if on cue, a thunderous roar filled the air as a bright light cut through the slats of the cabin walls. Cody sprang out of bed and rushed outside. He spotted two military helicopters hovering over the camp. Their searchlights raced over the grounds and their spinning rotors sent dirt and pine needles flying.

Cody spotted one of his instructors, Victor Diaz, running near the illuminated patterns. His instructor tightly grasped a backpack as he leapt back, trying to avoid the spotlights. Cody ran up to him.

"What's going on, sir?" asked Cody.

At first, Diaz seemed surprised to see him. Then his piercing eyes locked onto Cody's. "It's a drill," his instructor informed him. "It's a commando raid and I'm putting you in charge. Run the op!"

Cool! Cody thought. Then, back to business. "What's the enemy's objective?"

Diaz seemed to think for a moment. "Let's say . . . I'm the target," he said. "What do you do?"

"Protect the target at all costs," Cody replied quickly.

At once, he shoved his instructor into the bushes just as several commandos rappelled from the helicopters. Then Cody turned and saw his bunkmates pour out of the cabin.

"It's a simulation!" Cody shouted.

"Cool!" Bender replied. "What's the mission?"

"Protect Big Bear," said Cody, using his instructor's code name. "We need a plan to hold those guys off so I can get Big Bear out of here!"

"Got it!" said Bender.

Cody reached into the bushes and grabbed Diaz by the arm. Together they ran into the darkness.

Ryan turned to Bender. "A plan, a plan . . ." he said. "Think, think!"

They looked at each other with blank stares.

"I got nothing," said Ryan.

"Me neither," said Bender.

Five commandos, dressed in black and wearing night-vision goggles marched toward the boys. Bender roared as he rushed them. The lead commando grabbed him by the sweatshirt and held him above his head. Bender threw punches into the air to no avail.

"Uh . . . if you need me," Ryan said nervously, "I'll be hiding under my bed!" He ran back into the cabin.

The two helicopters had landed in an open field near the lake. One of the pilots was checking his instruments as his door suddenly flew open. Cody Banks reached in, ripped the pilot from his seat, and then pinned the pilot's arms to his side with an inner tube. Cody pushed him away with a kick, sending the pilot rolling down the hill toward the lake. Meanwhile, Diaz jumped into the now empty pilot's seat.

"I hope you can fly this thing," said Cody.

Diaz looked to his right. "What about the other chopper?"

"Trust me," Cody replied. "He's not going anywhere!"

Cody shut the door and stepped away from the helicopter, giving a "thumbs-up" to Diaz. His instructor grinned at him strangely as the helicopter lifted off.

Cody watched as the second helicopter began to give chase. As it took off, it lifted a long chain from the ground. The chain ran from the skid of the helicopter to the lake. As the helicopter flew higher, several buoys from the lake shot out of the water until the chain pulled taught. The second helicopter hovered like a balloon tied with a long string as Diaz's helicopter disappeared into the night.

Cody smiled. *Mission accomplished*, he thought.

Just then, a black Humvee barreled across the field toward him. Several commandos exited the surrounding tree line and approached as well. Cody was surprised to see the director of the CIA step out of the vehicle.

"Banks!" shouted the tall man as he stomped toward the boy. "What's going on? Where's Diaz?"

"By now?" Cody replied, "a long way from here."

The director's brow furrowed. "Do you have any idea what you've done?"

"Well, from the looks of things," replied Cody, "I'd say that I've just beaten your little simulation."

"There is no *simulation*!" the director yelled and pointed to the distant horizon. "That man just stole the single most dangerous device this country has ever developed and *you* helped him get away!"

Cody swallowed hard. "Not good," he said to himself. "Not good at all."

4

HIDDEN SECRETS

"There has to be some mistake." Cody ran to keep up as the director strode across the dining hall. "What's here for him to steal?"

"The CIA maintains a secret storage facility underneath this camp," the director replied curtly.

"That's impossible," Cody said. "Kids have been snooping around this place for years. Somebody would have found the entrance by now."

"We hid it in the one place no kid at summer camp would ever look," the man said, coming to a stop in front of . . .

"THE SALAD BAR?" Cody asked in disbelief.

The director held up a remote and pushed a button. The salad bar slid silently aside revealing a secret set of stairs leading down into darkness. Cody cautiously followed as the director stepped down the dark stairs. At the bottom, the man flicked a switch and hundreds of fluorescent lights revealed a huge industrial warehouse. Rows and rows of shelves, crates, and file cabinets seemed to go on for miles in the cavernous storage area.

"What *is* this stuff?" asked Cody as he followed the director down one of the many walkways.

"Stolen technology, weapons, obsolete inventions," the director replied.

Cody stopped and picked up a loud, plaid sport coat. Its bright mismatched colors were almost as hideous as its large pointed collar.

"That's your standard agency issue, combat polyester sport coat, very popular in the seventies," said the director. "It's completely bulletproof, fireproof, and the collar could be used as a flotation device."

Suddenly, the incredibly wide collar inflated like an airplane life jacket. Cody couldn't believe the jacket could be even more repulsive than before.

"Wow. I gotta have one of these," Cody said sarcastically.

He put the jacket down and followed the director around a corner.

"So Diaz stole a bunch of ugly jackets?" asked Cody.

"I wish," replied the director. "What do you know about mind control?"

"I know every country in the world's been trying to perfect it since forever," replied Cody.

The director stopped at the end of a long corridor. "It was the space race nobody talked about."

The director held out his remote, aimed it at the wall, and then pushed a button. A wall projector sprang to life and began projecting holographic footage of scientists working on mind-control prototypes.

Older footage showed several subjects wearing bulky backpacks and helmets. As the scenes progressed however, Cody saw scientists working on smaller, less obtrusive devices, then finally, microchips.

"Five years ago, Diaz oversaw a group of scientists working on the project," the director narrated. "We were close, but he was closer." He called out to the projector, "Run program."

The holographic images changed to the form of a burly, gray-haired man.

"Dr. Duncan Kenworth," said the director. "A British scientist always on the verge of bankruptcy until he married a rich widow a few years ago." The holographic image of Kenworth slowly rotated. "Now he has a God complex and sufficient funding to indulge it." Victor Diaz's image joined Kenworth's. The two men stood side-by-side.

"So, you think Diaz and Kenworth are working together?" asked Cody.

"Freeze image," said the director, taking a closer look at the image of Diaz. "We had developed five prototype chips but could never make them work," he said. "If anybody can finish the job it's Kenworth."

"So, I'm supposed to make sure he doesn't do that," said Cody. He grew excited at the thought of another secret mission.

"His wife, Jo Kenworth, runs a program where students live on their estate and attend the Hastings Academy of Music," the director added.

Cody's hopes fell. "More school?" he asked. "Just once I'd like a mission that doesn't involve homework." Then Cody shot the director a surprised look. "Wait a minute, did you say music?"

"Yes, you'll be part of an International Youth Orchestra," replied the director. "Good thing you play the clarinet,"

"Uh, sir . . ." Cody glanced around nervously. "I don't play the clarinet."

"What are you talking about?" The director looked at him in disbelief. "Your file said you were in the band for three years."

"Yes, I was in the band, but I never actually played," Cody sighed. "I faked playing to meet girls."

"You thought playing clarinet in the Marching Band was going to get you girls?" asked the director with a smirk.

"I was shy!" Cody said in his defense.

"You were delusional," the director replied.

"The point is," Cody continued, "I'm never going to be able to pull this off!"

"You faked it for three years, you can fake it for another couple of weeks," the director said. "All we have to do is convince your parents to let you go."

5

FOR THE LOVE OF MUSIC

"LONDON?!!" Cody's mother bellowed.

Cody followed his mother into the house. She had stopped thumbing through the day's mail when he told her the news. Cody's dad sat at the dining table sorting the monthly bills.

"It's an international youth orchestra," said Cody

"But you haven't played in years!" said his mother.

Cody gave a dramatic sigh. "I knew the lies would catch up with me sooner or later." He turned toward his dad. "Mom, Dad, this may come as a shock to you, but I never gave up my beloved clarinet."

"What?" asked his mom. She'd all but forgotten the mail in her hand.

"I've been playing in secret for years under an assumed name," Cody replied, reciting his well-thought-out story. "Weddings, polka festivals, seedy underground chamber music clubs. I'm not proud of it but I've done them all."

"I always assumed that you joined the marching band just to meet girls," said Mr. Banks.

Cody chuckled. "How pathetic would that be?" He turned back to his mother, "So, Mom, you'll let me go?"

Cody's mom seemed to be buying it. "Well, it does sound like a . . ."

"No!" his dad interrupted.

"But think of the educational opportunities," Cody said.

"I've got an opportunity for you. Weed the backyard." His dad thumbed over his shoulder, toward the back door.

"Come on Dad!" Cody pleaded.

"Forget it." Mr. Banks gestured to the pile of bills on the table. "I can barely afford to feed you in America."

"But you have to let me do this!" Cody demanded.

"No, your father's right," Mrs. Banks said, going back to sorting the mail. She gave a stack to Mr. Banks. "We just don't have the money."

"But that's the only reason, right?" asked Cody. "If we had some extra money you'd let me go to London and follow my . . . my . . . secret clarinet dreams?"

"Sure," his mother replied with a laugh. "But it's not as if money is going to fall from the sky."

"Money!" yelled Cody's father. He held a check and an opened envelope. "Look! A supplemental IRS refund!" He stood and displayed it for Mrs. Banks to see. "Eight-thousand, eight hundred and sixty-two dollars! We're rich!"

Cody glanced through the front window. He saw Bender standing beside the mailbox dressed as a mailman. The uniform sagged on him as he gave Cody a "thumb's-up" and disappeared down the sidewalk.

"I can't believe it!" cried Cody's father. "Almost nine thousand dollars!"

"Great! I'll go pack!" said Cody as he ran out of the room.

Confused, Cody's father looked up from the check. "Wait a minute," he said. "What just happened?"

Cody's mom smiled. "I guess Cody's going to London."

6

A NEW HANDLER

Carrying his two suitcases, Cody walked through the terminal of London's Heathrow International Airport. As soon as he stepped off the plane, he was greeted with the sights, sounds, and smells of another country. Signs displayed ads for products he didn't recognize, he smelled unfamiliar colognes and perfumes, and everyone spoke in a British accent.

Almost everyone.

"Fa shizzle dizzle," an American voice said. "It's the big Neptizzle."

Cody bent down and pretended to tie his shoe. Then he gave his part of the code. "When I pull up front, you see my Benz on dubs," Cody said quietly.

He gave a quick glance to a person sitting on a nearby bench eating fish and chips. He was a heavyset man trying way too hard to be inconspicuous.

"My flow, my show, brought me all this dough," the man continued.

Cody stood and walked toward him. "I got my mind on my money and my money on my mind," he said. "Some code you got there."

"I keep telling them," the man replied, looking up at the young agent. "It ain't hard to confuse the Chinese. All you gotta do is throw down a little Snoop Dog." Still eating, the man stood. "Agent Cody Banks, my name is Derek Burnett, your new handler." He looked Cody up and down. "I've heard a lot about you. And finally meeting you is . . . really disappointing."

"Excuse me?" asked Cody.

"You're a legend and look at you," Derek replied. "You'd get carded at Chuck E. Cheese." The man licked his fingers and held out the greasy container of chips, which were England's version of French fries. "Chip?"

Cody shook his head and walked toward the exit. He couldn't believe this was his new handler.

Derek threw his greasy container into a nearby trash bin and followed the young agent. "What did I say?" he asked.

Once outside, Derek led Cody to a black taxicab parked beside the curb.

"The Black Cab," said Derek. "A London icon. You see a million of them everywhere you go. They blend into traffic, you park them anywhere, and nobody gives you a second thought." Derek opened the back door. "Perfect cover for a state-of-the-art field unit," he said proudly.

Cody gazed into the cab's interior. It was filled to the brim with tons of high-tech equipment.

"I designed it myself," Derek continued. "It's got the Gucci interior, plasma flat screen, DVD, GPS, wireless Ethernet, and our driver, my right-hand man, Kumar." He gestured toward a man in the front seat.

"Pleasure, Mr. Banks," said Kumar. The brown-haired man gave Cody a wave, his mustache widening to reveal a smile underneath.

"And . . ." Derek said as he fished a remote from his pocket. "The best sound system in London." Derek grinned as a booming hip-hop song blared from the speakers.

"That's on 'two,'" Derek said proudly "If I crank it up to 'ten,' your internal organs just liquefy."

"Nice," replied Cody. "Of course every time you turn this on you risk blowing your cover and putting yourself and all your men in danger." Cody threw his bags into the cab and climbed inside.

Derek shook his head. "I know what this is about," he said. "You probably like country music."

Derek hopped in and Kumar drove them through the busy London streets. As they traveled along, Cody gazed out the window at the passing sights. London had the feel of New York with the historical presence of Washington D.C. The streets were crowded with people, shops, and office buildings yet the structures were much older than the ones he was used to. And even though Cody knew about it beforehand, it *was* a bit strange to actually see everyone driving on the left side of the road instead of on the right.

As they motored by Buckingham Palace, traffic became much worse. Police were setting up barricades in front of the immense structure and workers were hanging a huge banner reading "Children's Rights Now."

"What's going on?" asked Cody.

"It's the World Conference on Children's Rights," said Kumar. "Presidents, prime ministers, and ambassadors from twelve countries are here to talk about education, feed the poor . . . put kids on the streets . . ."

"Don't you mean, *off* the streets?" Cody asked.

"They're putting them somewhere," replied Kumar. "I'm not sure where."

Cody turned to Derek. "What can you tell me about Dr. and Mrs. Kenworth?"

Derek fished out a thin blue folder and handed it to Cody. He opened it to find photos of Duncan and Jo Kenworth as well as several documents listing information about the two.

"She's from a very rich family," Derek informed him. "They have no kids, because Dr. Kenworth hates them so much, which is probably why Lady Kenworth puts so much energy into her music program."

Cody closed the folder. "When do I meet the rest of your staff?" he asked Derek.

Kumar waved from the driver's seat.

Cody couldn't believe it. "This is our backup?" he asked. "One guy?"

Derek looked a little embarrassed. "Well the new *field unit* took up a bigger piece of the budgetary pie than I had previously anticipated."

"What was your last mission?" Cody asked skeptically.

"Oh, you want to check me out?" asked Derek. "Well, I'd love to play this game, but I can't really talk about it." He rubbed his chin thoughtfully. "Let's just say I was involved in a top secret, high priority, undercover, intelligence gathering project"

"At Starbucks," Kumar added from the front seat.

"Starbucks?" Cody asked in disbelief.

A bit flustered, Derek tried to recover. "You've obviously never spent any time there!" he said. "People get high on caffeine and spill their guts. We were able to dig up a lot of heavily classified information."

"We knew about the new mocha mint Frappucino months before anybody else," Kumar added proudly.

Derek shot him a dirty look. "You are not helping, you know."

Cody chuckled. "You must have really ticked somebody off to get an assignment like that."

"You're young." Derek glared at him. "One day you'll see that things don't always work out like you planned."

Derek and Kumar drove Cody to The London Dungeon, a large tourist attraction depicting the history of London's most infamous criminals and how they were punished. They boarded one of the boats that floated tourists through the exhibit, but they didn't finish the ride. Halfway through, they stepped off the boat and entered a secret doorway.

Okay, this is cool, thought Cody.

Once through the door, Cody saw what appeared to be the museum's repair room. Pieces of skeletons, guillotines, and other spooky artifacts lay about the room in various states of repair. A bookish-looking man wearing dirty overalls sat behind one of the worktables.

"Cody, this is Neville Stubbings," said Derek. "He works here at the museum but that's just a cover. He's one of us." Derek turned to the thin man. "Neville, you got a goody bag for my man here?"

"Right, let me see," said Neville. He reached under the table and pushed a secret button. A hidden compartment folded out from beneath the worktable revealing what appeared to be everyday items. "A few things you might find useful."

Neville produced a pack of breath mints. He removed a mint and licked one side. "All you do is take a quick lick, slap one on any conventional lock and you're in!"

Neville placed the damp mint onto the lock of a nearby cabinet. *POP!* The mint blew up in a tiny explosion. The cabinet door popped open and smoked billowed out.

"Unfortunately, if you accidentally eat one," Neville continued, "you'll be drinking through a straw to say the least."

"Now," Neville continued, "Recognize this?" The man held up a small object made of skin-toned plastic and wire. It was Cody's dental retainer. "We've turned your retainer into a personal listening device with directional capabilities." He pointed to the bottom of the retainer. "You manipulate range, volume, and intensity using your tongue."

Neville placed the retainer onto the worktable and then removed an ordinary belt from the compartment. "Next, your basic belt. Except that underneath the buckle I embedded a high-tension micro-cable." Neville aimed the buckle toward the opposite wall of the repair room. "Pop the highly recognizable designer logo, aim and . . ." A tiny arrowhead shot across the room trailing a thin wire. The sharp tip embedded itself into the far wall, knocking over a few test tubes and beakers.

"Fire," said Cody.

"Exactly!" Neville replied proudly. He glanced at the empty compartment. "Well, that's about all I have."

"No, I mean *fire*!" Cody repeated, pointing to the small flames erupting from the shelf of broken test tubes.

"Oh dear," said Neville as he rushed to put out the fire. He slapped at the flames with a nearby towel.

Ignoring Neville's efforts, Derek calmly turned to Cody. "Kumar will take you to Kenworth's." He glanced back at Neville. "I'll help him clean up."

"So, I guess this is good-bye," Cody said, extending a hand to Derek.

"Oh, you're not getting rid of me that easy," Derek replied. "I'll be around."

"Perfect," Cody said to himself as he followed Kumar toward the exit. He didn't feel very confident in his handler's abilities.

7

CODY'S NEW HOME

"This is just one house?" asked Cody as the cab pulled to a stop in the courtyard of a huge English castle. If he wasn't in England, he might have thought the immense mansion was big enough to belong to a movie or rock star.

"This is just one wing," Kumar remarked.

Cody stepped out of the car and gazed at the giant estate. The castle looked like the ones in almost every old movie he had seen. Huge moss-covered stones supported tall turrets. Crowded rooftops overlapped each other, and wide-mouth gargoyles pouted in corners acting as drain spouts. Cody half-expected Dr. Frankenstein to appear in the doorway. Instead, he saw a pleasant-looking older woman. He immediately recognized her from the photo in her file.

"My word! Cody Banks!" said a very excited Jo Kenworth. "Welcome to London!" She glided down the steps and took Cody's hand. "I would have picked you up at the airport myself, but quite frankly I forgot you were coming. I trust your crossing was pleasant?" she asked.

"Yes, I *crossed* just fine," said Cody.

Mrs. Kenworth ran back up the stairs. "I can't wait for you to meet the rest of the students." Just inside the doorway, she cupped her hands to her mouth. "Oh, children!" She glanced back to Cody. "I'll collect them and we'll meet in the library." Jo Kenworth disappeared through the castle doorway.

Cody grabbed his bags and trudged up the steps. Once inside, he took in his new lodgings. The ceiling seemed impossibly high, a grand stairway led upstairs, and priceless artwork and antiques were sprinkled throughout.

As Cody stepped deeper into this reproduction of a silent movie location, he noticed an open doorway just off the main hallway. Cody looked around, set down his bags, and snuck inside.

Cody guessed that this large room was Dr. Kenworth's study. His educated guess came from the fact that every wall was covered by self-portraits of the doctor. Everywhere he glanced, he saw Kenworth looking regal, Kenworth looking contemplative, and Kenworth in repose.

Cody whistled to himself. "Okay, looks as if somebody's a little stuck on himself."

"Maybe," said a voice behind him. "And yet, perhaps I have a greater goal in mind."

Startled, Cody spun around to see the real Dr. Kenworth in a corner of the room. The man stood before a mirror as he painted yet another self-portrait.

"Dr. Kenworth, I'm so sorry," Cody apologized.

"Maybe I'm trying to breathe life into a barren soul or seek redemption in an innocence lost," Kenworth mused. "Or maybe I just think I'm gorgeous."

"I'm sorry," Cody repeated. "I was out of line."

"Yes, you were," Kenworth replied as he stepped away from his latest work. "Do you consider every open door an invitation to blunder in and have a go around?"

"No, sir," said Cody.

Cody glanced at a nearby desk and saw some technical drawings and electronic schematics. Was this what the young agent was looking for?

Noticing the boy's gaze, Kenworth quickly covered the drawings with some blank pages and books. "Ever tried to paint someone's portrait?" asked Kenworth, changing the subject.

"Every year for Mother's Day until I was twelve," Cody said with a laugh. "Then she finally asked me to stop."

"It's not so hard in the abstract," said Kenworth. "Flesh and bone are just form and content, but the eyes?" He moved closer to Cody. "Capturing the eyes is the key to everything." He moved even closer. "They betray our darkest desires, don't you think?"

"Uh . . . yeah, eyes are good," Cody said nervously. He turned his attention to the surrounding study. "Exactly how many of these have you painted?"

"It is a little disarming at first, but you'll get used to me," said Kenworth. "I'm *everywhere*." He gave Cody a long, disturbing look.

Cody apologized again and quickly left the study. With his bags in tow, he managed to find the mansion's library. He stepped into the large room and gazed at its many book-lined shelves. The rest of the young musicians stood in the center. There were twelve different young boys and girls from many different nationalities and countries. Cody joined them.

"Oh, welcome, welcome!" shouted Mrs. Kenworth. "Seeing you all together for the first time is just smashing." She waved grandly toward Cody. "Children, this is Cody Banks."

"The American," said a boy with a French accent. "Now, we are but complete."

A young Pakistani girl rushed up to Cody. "Do you know Britney Spears?" she asked.

"Um . . . no, not really," replied Cody, surprised by the question.

"Sabeen loves Britney Spears and all things American," Mrs. Kenworth reported.

"Britney's main inspirations are Aretha Franklin and rainy days," Sabeen recited proudly.

"You really know your Britney," said Cody.

"Imagine her parents' pride," said Mrs. Kenworth. She pointed to a girl giving Cody a suspicious look. "And this is Emily, a local girl." She turned to the young girl. "Have you met Cody Banks?"

"Oh, he's not to be missed, that one," Emily said curtly.

"Lovely," Mrs. Kenworth replied, Emily's sarcasm flying right over her head. "I'll let you go in just a tick, but first, a few ground rules." A serious expression washed over the woman's face for the first time since Cody had met her. "I've worked hard to ensure that the reputation of this program is impeccable so you are expected to conduct yourselves in a proper manner." She pointed her finger at the group. "If I find you slacking off in either your musical preparations or your studies, you'll be sacked immediately." She placed her hands on her hips. "And I'll know, for I will be watching you at all times, understood?"

Everyone nodded. Cody realized it would be difficult for him to do any investigating.

"Now, that we got that out of the way." Mrs. Kenworth smiled again. "The World Conference on Children's Rights will conclude on Saturday and guess what youth orchestra will be playing for the queen?"

The other young musicians gasped and looked at each other in delight. Cody sighed. Since he could barely remember holding the clarinet, much less playing it, he knew of one kid who would actually be "faking it" in front of the queen.

"So, off to rehearse," Mrs. Kenworth ordered, shooing away the students. "You have a little time before dinner and I want music flowing from all your rooms. Scurry on!"

As the kids left the library, Cody grabbed his bags and followed. The French boy brushed hard past him, but young Sabeen was right by his side.

"How about any of those 'Survivor' persons?" she asked. "Ever met any?"

"Sorry," Cody replied as he carried his bags up the long staircase.

Sabeen sighed with disappointment. "You don't seem to get out much."

The young girl followed him down the hall, deluging him with questions along the way. Cody finally reached a room with his name printed on a small sign next to the door.

Cody turned to Sabeen. "I'm going into my room now. Alone." He opened the door and Sabeen began to follow him in. He quickly blocked her entry. "I'm going to close the door now, leaving you outside."

Cody quickly shut the door then listened for movement on the other side. For a moment, he didn't hear anything. Then he heard Sabeen's footsteps as she reluctantly walked away. Cody sighed and turned toward his room.

It was the largest bedroom he had ever seen. Several large antique dressers and cabinets stood against the walls, while the ceiling stretched high above him. The ceiling had to be high in order to fit the gigantic four-poster bed. *You could land a helicopter on that bed*, Cody thought.

Hearing a slamming door outside, Cody moved to the large window and leaned outside. Far below him, in the fading sunlight, he saw Dr. Kenworth speaking angrily into a cell phone.

Cody reached into his pocket and pulled out his newly modified retainer. He slipped it into his mouth. Cody moved his jaw from side to side, trying to find the 'on' switch, but nothing happened. Then he slid his tongue over the roof of his mouth and his ears were filled with deafening chaos.

Incredibly amplified, he heard the sound of crickets, a snoring cat, a squeaky gate, and leaves rustling in the trees.

"AHHH!" Cody screamed and quickly popped out the retainer.

Cody rubbed his ears, hoping they didn't sustain major damage. Then he gingerly placed the retainer back into his mouth and used his tongue to adjust the range and direction of the powerful microphone. He focused it in on Kenworth.

"I told you I never wanted to see you until . . ." Kenworth's voice faded as he started walking away. Cody readjusted the retainer. "Anyway, it's impossible," Kenworth continued. "This place is crawling with kids."

Then Kenworth's voice faded all together as he walked around a corner. Cody wondered to whom he was talking. He knew he had to hear the rest of this conversation.

So he hopped onto the windowsill then cautiously stepped out onto the ledge. He balanced himself carefully as he crept along the ledge toward a turn in the castle wall. Using the corner as leverage, he pushed off the wall with one foot and leapt for the roof above. With his fingertips holding firmly, Cody pulled himself onto the roof. The top of the giant estate was broken into various sections with roof levels in assorted heights and distances. Cody sprinted across the current section then dove into a back flip. The young agent flew over a ten-foot gap, landing safely on another section of roof. He listened to Kenworth as he passed.

"I don't have to explain myself to you!" Kenworth barked. "Suffice it to say, I don't want you over here. The estate is crawling with grimy children, getting into everything!"

Kenworth's voice faded once more as he continued his trek around the large building.

Cody looked ahead and saw a twenty-foot gap in front of him. It was way too far to jump. He reached down and removed his new belt.

Wrapping the belt around one arm, Cody aimed the buckle at a towering spire at the far end of the roof. The high-tension wire exploded from the buckle and lanced through the air. The sharp arrowhead embedded itself into the stone spire.

Cody took a running start then jumped over the large expanse. The wire tightened as he arced through the air. He couldn't believe how much fun he was having. So much so, that he didn't see the stone gargoyle racing toward him. He slammed into the silent beast and it knocked the wind out of him.

"Hold on a second," Kenworth said, looking up toward Cody.

The young agent stepped onto a nearby ledge and ducked into the shadows.

Dr. Kenworth stared a moment longer then turned his attention back to the caller. "It was nothing," he reassured. "I'm telling you, if you show up here I will . . . hello? Hello?" Kenworth slammed the phone shut in frustration. "Blast!" He stormed back the way he had come.

Cody stayed in the shadows until he left. Unfortunately, he hadn't discovered whom Kenworth was talking to, but he had a pretty good idea.

8

A MIDNIGHT STROLL

Beep-beep! Beep-beep!

Cody's watch chimed midnight and he hopped out of bed. At least, he tried to hop out of bed. With the large down mattress and thick blankets, he struggled just to poke his head out of bed much less climb out. He finally reached up, grabbed a decorative rope hanging from one of the bed's four posts, and slowly pulled himself out of the monstrous bed.

Being careful not to wake any of the other students, Cody slipped out of his room and padded down the hall. His destination: Dr. Kenworth's study. He had to get a better look at those plans.

Once he snuck into the study, he quietly moved to Kenworth's desk. The plans were gone. He searched nearby drawers and cabinets, but found no sign of the schematics he had seen earlier. His attention was quickly drawn to a locked cabinet beside the fireplace. He moved closer and reached into his pocket. One semi-moist breath mint should take care of the lock.

Suddenly, he heard a familiar noise in the hall outside. It was the sound of a bouncing racquetball. That sound meant only one thing: Diaz was there. His suspicions were confirmed when he heard his voice as well as Dr. Kenworth's.

"I told you not to come here!" Dr. Kenworth whispered angrily.

Cody watched as the two men entered the study.

"It's too risky," continued Kenworth. "Someone could have seen you."

"Doctor, Doctor, Doctor, twenty years in the CIA," Diaz reassured. "Nobody sees me unless I want to be seen."

That wasn't entirely true. Cody could see the two men, but they couldn't see him. He watched them on the view screen of his watch. Wedged inside the chimney, Cody extended a small video camera down the chimney and out of the fireplace.

"Okay, you're here now, what do you want?" asked Kenworth.

"What do I want? I want to know what's going on!" Diaz demanded. "I haven't heard anything from you since I gave you one of the prototypes." Diaz noticed the self-portraits hanging about the study. "Is this what you've been doing with your time?"

"What do you care?" Kenworth asked. "We agreed to a plan and I will not scupper it just because you're getting bored."

Cody adjusted his grip and accidentally dislodged a piece of stone. The small rock tumbled to the fireplace floor. Cody held his breath.

Startled, Diaz looked around the room. "What was that?"

Dr. Kenworth sighed. "The house dates back to the sixteenth century. I'm afraid it's a little noisy."

Cody breathed again.

"Are we done here?" asked Kenworth.

"Oh, I'm done with you," Diaz sneered. "Hand over the prototype."

Kenworth shook his head and removed a set of keys from his pocket. He unlocked the very cabinet Cody was trying to get into. "Oh, Victor, you're so impulsive." He removed a sophisticated-looking joystick. "It's going to prove fatal some day."

"Is that a threat?" asked Diaz.

"A threat? Of course not," replied Kenworth. "I was just going to offer you some tea."

Cody watched as a large dog wandered into the library. It trotted to a small tea table, picked up a teapot with its mouth and trotted over to Diaz.

"Wait a minute," Diaz said, surprised. "How are you doing this?"

Cody aimed the camera toward the dog. As the camera zoomed in on the canine, Cody saw a small blinking light on its collar. "It works," he whispered to himself.

Victor Diaz held out a small teacup. The dog tilted its head and poured tea into the awaiting cup.

"Okay, I'm impressed," Diaz admitted. "But will it work on humans?"

"Very tricky," replied Kenworth. "The human nervous system is

Banks.
Cody Banks.
Highly trained CIA operative.

Location: Kenworth Estate, London
Cover: International Youth Orchestra musician
Mission: retrieve stolen mind-control device

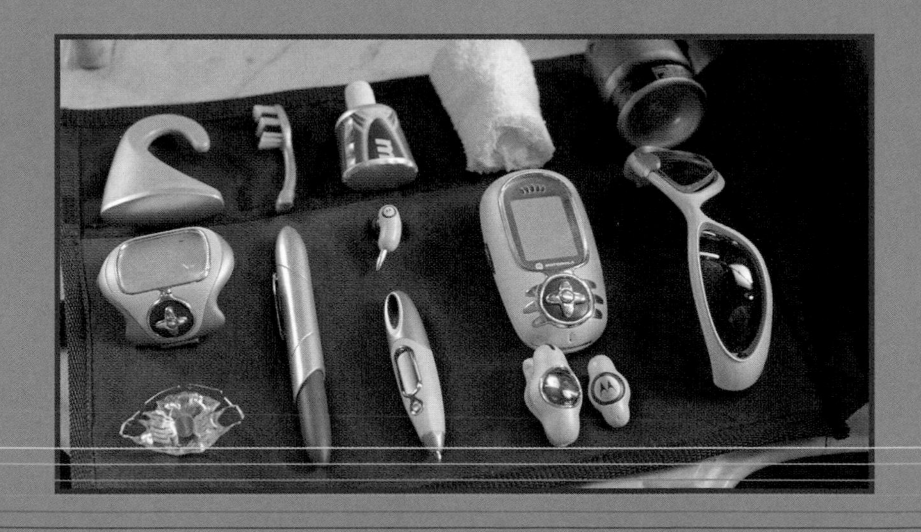

Location: Kenworth Laboratories
Objective: break into labs and locate missing device

Location: Buckingham Palace
Objective: create a distraction and apprehend suspects

Warning: Under no circumstance allow your cover to be compromised or you'll risk becoming brainwashed yourself!

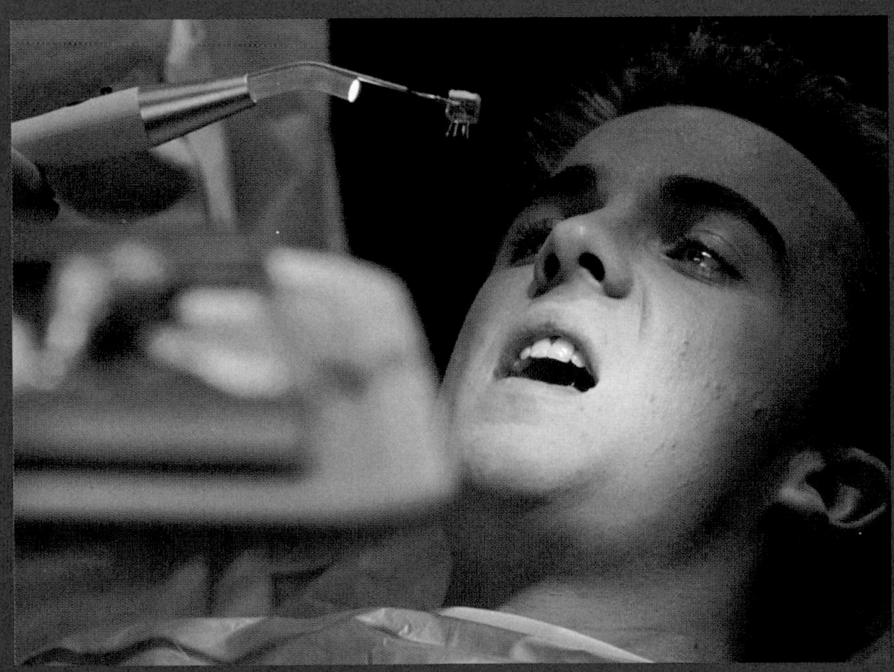

much more sophisticated. It'll take time. If you gave me the other prototypes . . ."

"Work with the one you've got," snapped Diaz. "Prove it works, then we'll talk."

"You don't trust me?" Kenworth asked with a sly smile.

"Of course not," Diaz leaned closer to the doctor. "I know you."

Diaz looked down to see that the dog had continued to pour long after the cup was full. Hot tea spilled over Diaz's hand and shoes. Cody's former instructor quickly set down the cup and flicked his hand.

"Well, what do you expect," Kenworth chuckled. "He is, after all, a dog."

After the two men left, Cody shimmied out of the fireplace and ran back to his room. So Diaz and Kenworth were in it together, and more importantly, Kenworth had found a way to make the mind-control prototype work — on dogs at least. But if it worked on a dog now, humans wouldn't be far behind. He had to sneak into Kenworth's lab tomorrow.

Cody crept down the hallway and eased open his bedroom door. He would soon be safe in his room and no one would be the wiser. What Cody didn't see was the door to Emily's room across the hall. As he stepped into his room, Emily peeked out of hers — watching him.

9

PLAYING THE CLARINET

Flomp!

The lunch lady slapped a spoonful of unidentifiable food onto Cody's tray. He looked down and decided that after seeing lunch at the Hastings Academy of Music, the food at his cafeteria back home didn't seem so bad.

"Eat up, Love," the lady chimed.

Cody smiled politely and carried his tray to an empty table. Then his cell phone rang. He quickly set down his food and answered.

"Banks," Cody said into the phone.

"I made some calls," Derek said on the other end of the call. "Apparently, Kenworth's staff at the lab takes some kind of Union 'crumpet break' at 2:15. Security's light about then so you should be free to roam around."

"Okay, swing by the school at two," replied Cody. "I'll be out front."

Cody switched off the phone and looked up to see Emily standing before him.

"Hi," Cody said nervously.

"What's happening at two?" asked Emily, eyebrows raised.

"Um . . . doctor's appointment," replied Cody.

"Really? What's wrong with you?" she asked.

"Uh . . . lung infection," Cody answered quickly. "Don't worry. It's not contagious or anything."

"A non-contagious lung infection?" Emily asked skeptically.

"It's an American thing," said Cody.

"Baseball, apple pie, and non-contagious lung infections," Emily recited.

"So, what do you think about the Kenworths?" Cody asked, trying to change the subject. "Especially, him. Weird guy, huh?"

"A little," Emily answered quickly. "You know, you look familiar, haven't I seen you somewhere before?"

"Maybe, I've been somewhere before," Cody answered even faster. "Ever notice anything weird around the house? People coming and going at strange hours? The dog mowing the lawn? Anything?"

"Can't say that I have," Emily retorted with lightning speed. "I've always heard brass instruments are hard to master is that true?"

"I wouldn't know since the clarinet is a woodwind," Cody replied. "But you knew that, didn't you?"

"I know a lot of things. You ask a lot of questions, don't you?" Emily quickly asked.

"Only when I don't know the answers," replied Cody. He shook his head. "Stop it! I can't keep talking like this. Why are you on my case?"

"You're the one who started it," Emily claimed.

"I'm just making idle conversation and from the looks of things, it's not like you've got a lot of other options," Cody jabbed. But as soon as the words were out of his mouth, he felt horrible for saying them.

Emily pursed her lips and turned away.

"Look, I didn't mean . . ." Cody began.

"We're late for rehearsal," Emily barked as she stomped away.

Outside the rehearsal hall, Cody could hear the other kids tuning their instruments. He had twenty minutes before he had to be outside to meet Derek. There was no time to make excuses to the teacher, he would just have to ditch the class altogether.

He turned and headed for the stairwell, then a hand clamped down on his shoulder.

"Young man?" a voice said.

Cody turned and saw the school's headmaster. The tall gray-haired man looked at Cody over the rims of his thin eyeglasses.

You're new here," the headmaster said, inspecting the young agent. "Don't you have someplace to be?"

"Yes, sir, right through those doors," Cody answered. "Got it covered. Just about to go in."

"See to it that you do, straight away," said the Headmaster. "I will not allow lackers in my hallways."

"No, lacking going on here, sir," Cody assured.

The headmaster casually walked down the hallway. With every other step, he looked back at Cody, suspiciously. The young agent realized that he had to go in. But everyone in there was expecting him to play. How would he get out of this one?

Just then, he saw a trash can by the door. When the headmaster wasn't looking, Cody dropped his clarinet case into the trash and opened the door. He smiled at his problem-solving skills.

Once inside, he saw the rest of the music students seated in front of their conductor, Maestro Hans Jerkovitch.

"Ah, Cody Banks, the clarinetist," said Maestro Jerkovitch. "We were going to send a search party out for you."

The other students allowed themselves a small chuckle. Cody fidgeted nervously.

"Maestro, I'm sorry I . . ." Cody began.

"I know." The maestro flicked back a strand of his long blonde hair. "You're honored to be in my presence and undeserving of such a unique gift."

"Wasn't exactly where I was going, but . . . okay," said Cody.

"Take your place," the maestro snapped. "We just got started moments ago and already I'm thinking of impaling myself on this baton."

"Um, Cody," Emily said in a melodic tone, "you seem to have forgotten your instrument."

"No, actually," stammered Cody, "tragically . . . it was stolen!"

The students gasped.

"Can you believe it?" asked Cody.

"I guess one mustn't leave his 'kazoo' lying around," said the French student, Marcel.

"That's really funny," said Cody. He turned to the maestro. "So, until I can have my spare shipped in from Seattle, I thought for the next few days, I could see the sights, take in some culture . . ."

"Hey, look what I found in the trash can outside!" said Sabeen

Cody spun around to see Sabeen standing by the door. His heart sank as he saw that she held his discarded clarinet case.

"Excellent," said the Maestro. "It seems your musical career has been miraculously revived."

"Yeah," Cody said without enthusiasm. He ripped the case from Sabeen's hands and took a seat with his fellow clarinet players.

The maestro tapped his baton on the podium. "Class, I have a most wonderful surprise. Our benefactor, Lady Jo Kenworth!"

The maestro gestured to a side room where Mrs. Kenworth walked through the open doors. She waved to the applauding students. Cody couldn't believe it.

"Maestro Jerkovitch," said Mrs. Kenworth, "I wonder if you could indulge me for just one moment."

"Consider yourself indulged," the maestro replied with a grand bow.

"Young Banks is one of the lads staying with me and well," she said, pointing to Cody. "I'm embarrassed to say I have yet to have the honor of hearing him play."

Cody's face warmed as all eyes turned to him. "I would hate to take up valuable rehearsal time," he muttered.

"Banks are you going to play something for us or not?" asked Maestro Jerkovitch.

Cody looked around. His mind raced. He couldn't think of a way out of it. He would have to play something.

Cody stood and slowly raised the clarinet to his lips. *Okay, okay, I must remember something, right?* he asked himself. *After three years of band, something had to have sunk in.*

Cody closed his eyes and began to play. Then he heard the most beautiful music in his life. Cody opened his eyes and was shocked to realize that the music was coming from his clarinet. Soft and haunting, it was the kind of music that breaks your heart and lifts your spirit at the same time.

When the song was over, everyone looked at Cody with jaws dropped. Then the entire class broke into thunderous applause. Nearby clarinet players slapped him on the back and shook his hand. Even Maestro Jerkovitch seemed impressed.

"That, I must say," the maestro admitted, "did not at all suck."

Cody couldn't believe it himself. "It's like a bicycle," he said, "I guess you never for . . ."

Before he could finish, the clarinet began to play the same beautiful tune. Realizing it was a special CIA clarinet, Cody quickly put mouthpiece to his lips. His fingers fumbled for the "off" switch.

"Banks, you have proven your mettle, may we continue?" asked the maestro.

While pretending to play, Cody's fingers still searched for the hidden switch. But that wasn't his only problem. He looked up at the clock. It was already two o'clock! He had to get out of there and meet Derek.

Finally, he hit the switch and the clarinet stopped playing. The other students, who once looked at him with amazement, now looked at him in disbelief.

"Excellent," said the maestro. "Now, from the top let us . . ."

Cody grabbed his nose. "Uh-oh, nosebleed!

He set down his clarinet and ran from the practice hall. Once outside, he stopped to take a breath. "Wow," he said to himself. "I can't believe that worked!"

10

LAB RESULTS

Derek parked the cab across the street from Kenworth Laboratories. Aside from the fact that it was in downtown London, Cody thought it looked much like any modern office building in the United States. He peered through the large windows in the front and spotted a lone security guard sitting behind a high reception desk.

Cody turned to Derek. "So, how am I supposed to get inside?"

"We'll need a foolproof plan," replied Derek.

"Which we don't have?" asked Cody.

"Nah," Derek confirmed. "I figured we'd wing it."

Derek and Cody walked through the front door of the building. Derek headed straight for the security guard. Cody crouched behind Derek so the guard wouldn't see him.

"Hey, this is a lab, right?" Derek asked the security guard. "Okay, I need one of those urine tests."

The guard looked up, not knowing what to say.

"Can you believe it?" Derek continued. "I go to work drunk *one* day, run over my boss's foot with a fork lift, and suddenly I've got a problem."

As Derek approached the desk, Cody jumped out from behind him, dropped to his knees, and slid past the desk and underneath the guard's view.

"Sir, I'm going to have to ask you to leave," the security guard said.

Derek crossed his arms. "Oh, you say this lab is too good to take my pee?"

"I assure you," the guard replied, "the quality of your . . . *pee* has nothing to do with it."

As soon as Cody passed the guard's desk, he popped up, walked toward the large entry doors, and slipped inside.

"I got cash," Derek continued behind him. "Now hand me a cup and let's do this thing."

Cody walked down a short corridor, stepped through another set of doors, and found himself on the floor of the main lab. He quickly snatched a lab coat from a nearby cubicle and slipped it on to blend in with other researchers. He worked his way through the large room, unnoticed.

Huge experiment stations were set up throughout the room. Cody saw experiments on everything from Cryogenics to optic implants. He stopped to watch one demonstration for some sort of sonic taser being developed for law enforcement.

A heavily shielded lab technician aimed the gun at a brick wall at the end of a long corridor. The taser screeched as it shot ripples through the air and blasted a hole through the wall.

"I don't believe it," Cody said, amazed.

Not seeing anything that resembled mind-control devices, Cody carefully made his way to the back of the lab. There, he crept through another door and into a long hallway. He then slipped an earpiece out of his shirt collar and placed it into his ear.

"I'm in," Cody said to Derek and Kumar. They were back in the cab following his movements on their tracking system.

"That's a go, Cody," said Derek. "Where are you?"

"In a hallway outside the main testing lab," Cody replied. "Near the big double doors."

Cody heard fingers tapping on a keyboard as Derek tried to pinpoint his position. "What double doors?" asked Derek.

Cody removed the lab coat and placed it on a nearby janitor's cart. He sprinted to the large doors. "You know, the double doors with the . . ." Cody stopped when he reached the doors. ". . . heavy locks and extra security that probably doesn't show up on any official blueprints."

Cody reached into his pocket and pulled out his special breath mints. He popped one out, licked its side, and slapped it onto the door's lock. After a quick flash, the lock was disabled. He cautiously opened the door and stepped in.

Cody found himself in yet another hallway but this one was shorter with three doors. He opened one; it was a conference room. He tried another — a storage closet. He was about to try the third one when it suddenly opened outward. Cody ducked behind the door and watched two men emerge. One man held a small, remote control. He toggled small joysticks as the other man seemed to be blindly following the first man.

As the two men exited through the double doors, Cody managed to grab the door they came out of before it closed.

This time Cody found himself in a large lab, which seemed to be dedicated to a single purpose. Several plasma screen monitors and equipment filled the area. And pinned to the walls, Cody saw blueprints for the mind-control prototype.

He turned his gaze to a large round table in the center of the room. On the table were different kinds of teeth, bridgework, and dental molds.

"What in the world?" Cody asked himself.

He then spotted a video camera set up on a tripod beside some nearby monitors. Cody hit a button on the camera and the monitors sprang to life. They showed the two men he had just seen exit the lab. The man with the remote control was talking to the man that was following him. Except now, that man sat at a table. The man nodded, then tried to pick up a pen on the table. Suddenly, his hand began to shake.

"What the . . . ?" Cody began, as he leaned forward for a closer look.

Unfortunately, he felt his leg brush up against something, heard a faint click, and then a loud siren. He must have tripped an alarm.

Cody dashed toward the exit, but it was too late. Large metal bars slammed down in front of the door.

"Guys," Cody said, "we've got a problem!"

He heard Derek and Kumar on the other end. "The man needs a back door," said Derek. "What do we got?"

More tapping from the keyboard. "Crawl space," Kumar replied.

Derek spoke loudly in his earpiece. "Cody, I need you in the ceiling!"

Cody looked up and saw an electrical access panel in the corner of the room.

"Got it!" Cody shouted.

He sprinted toward the corner and jumped at the wall. He pushed off with one foot to the other wall then leapt back and forth using the two walls like a ladder. Then he grabbed one of the steel beams running across the ceiling. He hung upside down from the beam and shimmied out to the access panel. Cody kicked it open and flung himself up inside. Once inside, Cody crawled through the ventilation system as fast as he could.

"Cody, do you see a vent leading to the outside?" asked Derek through the earpiece.

Cody turned a corner and saw light streaming though the gratings of a large vent. "Yeah!"

"Head toward it," Derek instructed. "We're on our way!"

Cody crawled faster.

Back in the lab, Kenworth and Diaz ran into the security room. Several monitors displayed various parts of the building. They focused on the monitor showing the mind control lab and found it vacant. However, when Kenworth rewound the grainy footage from the VCR recording all activity in the lab, he saw a young figure.

"Wait a minute," said Diaz. "Right there, freeze it!"

They both stared at the frozen image of Cody Banks looking right at the camera.

"My word," Kenworth gasped. "That's one of the musician kids staying at the estate. Um, Cody . . ."

"Banks," Diaz finished.

Surprised, Kenworth turned to Diaz. "You know him?"

The ex-CIA agent tightened his lips. "I know he's no musician."

Cody slammed the vent with his fist. The metal grating clattered as it fell into the alley. The young agent somersaulted out of the opening just as the black cab screeched to a stop beside him. A door flew open and Cody jumped in. Derek hit the gas and the cab took off.

"Not bad, huh?" Derek asked proudly. "Think they can mess with Derek Burnett? Not today!"

"They're experimenting on people," Cody reported.

"What?" Derek asked as he whipped in and out of traffic.

"The mind-control prototype!" exclaimed Cody. "They're testing it on people!"

"Does it work?" asked Derek. He turned the wheel just in time to miss a group of pedestrians.

"I don't . . ." Cody looked up and saw a huge double-decker bus barreling toward them. "Slow down!" he yelled. "What are you doing? Are we being chased?"

"No, worse!" Derek replied, pressing down on the accelerator. "You're late for class!"

11

SONIC BOOM

After school, the music students filed onto a bus to take them back to the Kenworth Estate. The sun was going down and the thickening fog made it seem later than it was. Emily and Cody were the last in line for the bus. Emily was about to board when she gave a curious look back at Cody. He didn't move toward the bus.

"Go on," said Cody. "I'll catch a cab."

"What are you talking about?" Emily asked.

Cody looked over his shoulder. "I have to do something."

"If you don't show up at Kenworths for evening meal, you'll be sacked for sure," Emily assured him.

"Don't worry," Cody replied. "I'll be there."

Emily climbed aboard and made her way to the back of the bus. As they pulled away, she eyed Cody suspiciously through the window.

Cody glanced across the darkening street to where Derek was parked. The young agent's handler was busy with a debate of his own.

"I said I'm off duty," Derek told the older gentleman trying to open the cab door. He leaned out of the driver's window. "You invented the language you'd think you'd understand." The man finally threw up his hands and walked away. Derek looked up and noticed Cody standing on the sidewalk. "Why didn't he get on the bus?" he asked himself.

Cody casually nodded toward a man standing near the school entrance. Cody had spotted him earlier, but he wanted to make sure the other kids were out of harm's way before he made a move. "We've got company," Cody whispered into his microphone.

The man in the shadows bounced a ball once then slowly backed into a dark alley.

"I see him," Derek replied through Cody's earpiece.

"I'm going to walk around the block and he'll follow me," Cody instructed. "You drive up behind him and we'll box him in."

"Got it," Derek replied.

Cody nonchalantly ambled passed the alley. He made sure not to turn around when he heard a very recognizable sound — the same sound he had heard back in Kenworth's lab right before something very bad happened.

Suddenly, Cody dove around the corner just as the ripples from a sonic taser ripped through the air and demolished a corner of the school building. Cody sprinted down the street and heard Diaz running behind him.

Derek peeled away from the curb after them. As he left, Kumar ran out of the nearby bushes, zipping his pants.

"Hey!" Kumar shouted.

Derek tried to turn down the street after Cody, but a garbage truck backed into his way.

"Move it!" Derek shouted out the window.

Cody dashed into another alley. He wove back and forth, making a clear shot impossible for Diaz. It didn't seem to help much. He watched as a rippled blast fired above him and demolished an overhead fire escape. Cody was then showered by pieces of scrap metal.

The young agent quickly pushed through an old door to his right. He dove down a set of rickety stairs just as another blast shattered the door behind him.

Cody crashed into a crate of vegetables and other supplies. With pieces of lettuce falling from his head, Cody stood, ran up the opposite set of stairs and into the store above. He zipped past the curious customers and tore through the front door and onto the sidewalk.

Diaz came around the corner, trying to cut him off.

Cody took a hard right and ran toward a crowded outdoor café. Rather than try and navigate through the congested patrons, Cody jumped onto the nearest table, then used the other tables as steppingstones to get to the other side. People yelled as he stepped on plates and knocked over glasses. He would have apologized if it weren't for the loud footfalls behind him. Diaz was closing the gap.

Cody leapt from the last table and landed in front of a flower shop. He ducked as he heard the sonic taser fire again. The shop window exploded and flower petals fell like snow as the young agent scrambled to his feet and kept running.

Cody turned into another alley. As he ran, he wondered where

Derek was. His handler was supposed to be right behind him, boxing Diaz in. Now he was doing his best not to be blasted by the sonic taser. Cody realized that *he* was now the one being boxed in as he ran down the alley.

Dead end.

Cody found himself facing two wooden gates blocking his escape from Diaz. He turned and saw Diaz raise the taser to shoot again. There was nowhere to run.

Diaz fired.

12

AN UNSETTLING DISCOVERY

Crash!

Driving a moped, Derek crashed through the wooden gate and grabbed Cody around the waist. The rippling taser fire zipped by Cody, blasting a hole through the other gate. Derek's moped slammed into the alley wall.

"Sorry," Derek apologized. "I had to find another ride."

"Nice one," Cody said as he got to his feet.

The two agents scrambled through the new hole and into an abandoned construction site. With Diaz behind them, they ran in and around partially constructed walls. After a few turns, Derek stopped Cody.

"What are we running for?" Derek asked. "We can take this guy. We should stand and fight!"

Cody heard the sound of the taser warming up. He grabbed

Derek by the shirt and yanked him down. The sheetrock wall exploded inches from where Derek's head was.

"After you," Cody said, gesturing to the fresh hole.

The two agents continued to run through the maze of walls and pipes as they worked their way deeper into the construction site.

"You know where you're going?" Derek asked between breaths.

"Of course not," said Cody.

"Well, that's good to know," replied Derek.

Dashing through open doorways, and around newly constructed walls, they made their way to the center of the open site. Cody now had no idea where Diaz was or how to get out of there.

Derek threw up his arms. "Great we're trapped."

Cody reached for his watch. "Maybe not."

"What's that?" asked Derek.

"It's a satellite watch," Cody said as he pressed a few buttons. "Standard agency issue."

"Standard nothing," Derek said angrily. "Mine doesn't even give the date!"

As Cody adjusted his watch, he heard a familiar voice.

"It's you isn't it, Banks?" Diaz asked. He was closer than Cody thought. "Of course it is. The irony is so thick it's almost cliché. Sending the pupil to catch the teacher."

Derek shot a look to Cody. "You know this guy?"

"He was my instructor," Cody replied. He called out to Diaz. "I thought you'd be flattered!"

"Oh, far from it," Diaz chuckled. His voice was even closer.

"The best they can send after me is a boy and a washed-up traitor who sold out his own country?"

Shocked, Cody looked at Derek.

"It's not what he . . . I didn't . . ." Derek stammered. He pointed to Cody's watch. "Just get us out of here, okay?"

Cody punched another button and his watch face faded away. It was quickly replaced by real-time video showing an infrared view of the construction site, both him and Derek, and Victor Diaz lurking a few rows away.

"I gotta get me one of those," Derek said, amazed.

Cody watched as the image of Diaz spun around and aimed the taser in their direction. He must have heard Derek's comment. The two agents split up as the wall exploded between them.

"They're using you. Don't you see that?" Diaz remarked, his voice more clear through the fresh hole. "You don't see, do you? It's addictive — the excitement, the danger. This starts to feel like real life and the rest of it doesn't seem to matter much anymore." Diaz's voice grew louder. "Yeah, it's changed you. Bit by bit, summer after summer, I could see it happening."

Cody crept down another half-finished corridor. The dust from the explosion, mixed with the growing fog, made it difficult to navigate. Cody tried to circle around while his former instructor kept talking.

"Give up, Cody," Diaz continued. "Turn around, walk out of here with your so-called partner and you won't get hurt. That's fair, don't you think? What do you say?"

Cody turned a corner and saw the back of Diaz. The young agent sprinted toward him. Diaz turned just as Cody pounced. The older man tried to aim the taser, but it was too late. Cody landed a powerful kick onto Diaz's chest, leveling the former agent. Diaz fell one direction, the taser slid the other.

"I say you're going to jail," said Cody.

Diaz immediately sprang to his feet. He launched a kick at Cody's face, which the young agent blocked. Diaz then attacked with a series of martial arts punches and kicks, which Cody blocked as well. Cody retaliated with moves of his own, but Diaz blocked them too. They seemed evenly matched.

"Not bad," Diaz remarked.

"I had a good teacher," Cody replied. "Too bad he was insane."

Diaz faked a punch and Cody went for it. Diaz spun around and landed a kick onto Cody's chest. The young agent was thrown back onto the ground and Diaz seized the moment to pick up his taser.

"You should've run when you had the chance," Diaz said as he leveled the gun on Cody.

Suddenly, Derek burst through a flimsy wall. He stomped onto a metal paint can lid that was propped on a wooden beam. The round lid twirled into the air, Derek caught it, and then whipped it like a Frisbee right at Diaz. The lid struck the former agent's arm, throwing off his aim. The taser blasted a hole into a wall instead of into Cody.

Just then, the entire construction site was lit like daytime. A police helicopter hovered overhead. The three dashed away in different directions. They would have to finish this another time.

* * *

Cody pushed hard on the sewer grate. Reluctantly, it slid aside. The young agent reached up and pulled himself out of the city street. He was almost clear when he heard footsteps.

"Derek, is that you?" he asked.

Suddenly, a number of flashlight beams blinded Cody's eyes. Through the glare, he made out the uniforms of several police officers.

"I guess not," Cody said with a sigh.

13

ALL IS NOT AS IT SEEMS

Cody sat quietly in the sparse interrogation room. There was only one door, a table, two chairs, a phone, and a large mirror. Cody waved at the mirror, sure it was a two-way surveillance device.

The door opened, and a tall, thin man stepped in. He seemed quite at home and dramatically paced across the room as if it were a stage. He placed the contents of Cody's pockets onto the table in front of him.

"I'm Inspector Rowland Crescent," the man said, "but I'm sure you already knew that."

"Uh, no," Cody replied.

"Really?" The inspector seemed surprised. "Well enough about me, let's talk about you." He picked up a credit card from the table. "Starting with this stolen credit card!"

"It's not stolen," Cody protested. "My dad gave it to me in case of emergencies."

"Ah, your *dad*?" the inspector seemed pleased. "Is that some clever code word for your accomplice?"

"No, it's the clever word I call my father." Cody sat back in his chair. "Look, this is a waste of time. Any second, that phone's going to ring and I'm walking out of here."

The man laughed. "Wishful thinking, I'm sure." The inspector nonchalantly strolled toward the large mirror and adjusted a few stray hairs. "You know, Banks, this can go two ways: easy, hard or . . . okay, three ways: easy, hard, or extremely . . ."

The phone rang, interrupting the inspector's well-rehearsed speech.

Cody smiled. "I think that's for you."

Inspector Crescent huffed over to the phone and answered. "Crescent, here." He suddenly snapped to attention. "I'm interrogating him right now." He paused and then stamped his foot. "But it's going so well." He reluctantly nodded his head. "Right away, of course."

Crescent hung up the phone and turned to Cody. "You're free to go," he said. "It seems you have some extremely powerful friends."

The inspector opened the door as Cody shoved his belongings into his pockets. The man then led Cody down a corridor and opened an office door. He motioned Cody inside.

Cody stepped into the fancy office and the door closed behind him. He saw the back of a high-back chair behind the large oak desk in the center of the room. Whoever was sitting there must have been gazing at the view of the London skyline.

"I guess I should thank you," Cody said.

When the chair spun around, Cody couldn't believe who was

sitting there. It was Emily. She wore a smart-looking suit and her hair was pulled back in a professional manner. For being the last person he expected to see, Emily fit right in to the office setting.

"Yes, you probably should thank me," she replied.

"Emily, what are you . . . ?" Cody stammered.

"You Americans, you always think you're one step ahead of the world," Emily said as she stood. "I've been on this case for months and you blunder in and almost blow the whole thing in a matter of days."

Still dumbfounded, Cody stared as she walked past him and opened the office door. "Let's get out of here," she suggested.

Cody sat across from Emily as they had a late dinner in a charming little restaurant. Cody could barely eat as he stared at his dining companion. The fact that she was more than just an annoying music student was still sinking in.

"My father was Military Intelligence," she explained. "I have an extensive martial arts background and I speak three languages. I was an obvious recruit." She sipped her soda. "And you?"

Cody snapped back into the conversation. "My father sells couches, I was a forward on the basketball team and I made a 'C' in English." He shrugged his shoulders and smiled.

"Quite the skill set you've got there," Emily remarked.

"It works for me," Cody grinned.

After another bite of her dinner, Emily got down to business. "So, why are you here? What does the American CIA want with Duncan Kenworth?"

"You go first," Cody replied.

"Kenworth has his lab working overtime on some top priority project," Emily explained. "He's been working with some American but we can't properly identify him or what they're up to."

Cody swallowed a sip of water then filled in the blanks. "He's working with ex-CIA Agent Victor Diaz to develop a mind-control device."

Emily dropped her fork. "My God, if it works . . ."

"It does," Cody announced. He took another bite and smiled. "I could use your help."

Emily smiled back. "You mean, I could use yours."

After dinner, Cody and Emily walked down a busy sidewalk. Other teenagers filled the walkway and lights from the clubs and shops glared off the wet cobblestone streets.

Emily pulled a package of mints out of her pocket and popped one into her mouth.

Cody panicked. "What are you doing?"

He reached a finger into her mouth and ripped out the candy. He tossed it into an alley and waited for the explosion. It never came.

"Are you mad?!" asked Emily.

Cody subtly felt the outside of his pants pocket. He realized that he still had his *special* breath mints.

"Uh, they're bad for your teeth," Cody replied. "Everybody knows that."

Emily gave him a strange look. "You're an odd one." She turned and waved a hand to the busy street. "Taxi!"

"Emily," Cody began, "this life, does it ever get to be, I don't know, too much?"

"It's a job, Cody, not your life." Emily gestured to a group of nearby teenagers. They stood around laughing and having a good time. "*This* is life. You can't forget that. You're no good to one without the other."

Cody gazed at the other kids enjoying themselves while Emily ran across the street after a cab. Maybe she was right. Maybe he was trying to grow up too fast. Maybe he needed to spend more time having a simple life, having fun with his friends, and generally just . . . being a kid.

Cody was lost in thought as a large black sedan screeched to a stop in front of him. The back door opened and a pair of arms reached out and grabbed him. They jerked him into the car and sped away.

14

CODY GETS DRILLED

Cody slowly woke but kept his eyes shut. He wasn't sure what had happened. One minute, he was standing on the streets of London, the next, he had a powerful headache and swore he heard elevator music.

Cody slowly opened his eyes. He found himself sitting in a dentist chair, in a dentist's office. He tried to move then realized he was strapped in. That explained the headache. The people in the black car must have drugged him after they grabbed him.

A man stepped into Cody's view. It was the man from the lab — the one leading the other man around with the remote control.

"He's awake," the man said.

Then Victor Diaz stepped into Cody's view. He looked at the other man, ignoring Cody Banks.

"Well, Walther, are you going to do this or not?" asked Diaz.

Walther glanced at Cody nervously. "He's just a kid!"

"So?" Diaz chuckled.

"You didn't tell me we were going to do kids," Walther replied. "I won't do it. I absolutely refuse."

Diaz picked up a wicked-looking dental tool from the nearby tray and pointed it at Walther. "Do it or I'll scoop out your liver!"

Walther immediately grabbed the drill and turned to Cody. "Say, Ahhh."

Cody struggled against the restraints but it was no use. He was wrapped up tight. Diaz grabbed his jaw and forced his mouth open. Walther leaned in and drilled away at one of Cody's teeth. After an agonizing moment, the man stopped and put his instrument away.

Diaz smiled at the young agent. "You know, if you put up a fuss you won't get a lollipop."

Too angry to worry about the pain, Cody glared at his former instructor. "It's not too late, Diaz. Come quietly now and I'm sure I can get you . . ."

"Rinse," Walther interrupted.

Cody turned his head to the side and spit in the nearby bowl. He turned back to Diaz. ". . . some kind of deal."

"Four or five hundred million dollars?" Diaz asked. "Because that's the kind of deal I have in mind."

"Whatever you're up to, you'll never get away with it," Cody warned. "They'll catch you for sure."

"No," Diaz replied. "They'll catch *you*."

Diaz grabbed Cody's jaw and forced it open once more. Walther leaned in and reached into Cody's mouth. The young agent felt a stab of pain as Walther did something to the tooth he drilled earlier. He heard a click then . . .

. . . blackness.

15

MORE THAN A TOOTHACHE

Cody slowly opened his eyes. He saw the top of his poster bed and the high ceiling of his room. He was back at the Kenworth Estate. There was another memory in his mind but it was fading fast. It was as if he had a nightmare that night, but couldn't remember what it was. Everything seemed fine now, though.

Cody rolled over and was startled to see Derek sitting in a nearby chair, staring at him.

"This room is bigger than my house!" Derek said.

Cody stumbled out of bed. The back of his head throbbed a little, but the pain seemed to be fading as fast as the nightmare.

"Where were you last night?" Cody asked.

"What are you talking about? We got separated in the construction site," Derek answered. "Scotland Yard picked you up and by the time I got there, you were gone." He gave Cody a curious look. "How'd you get home?"

Cody thought a moment. How *did* he get home? "Taxi, I guess," he told Derek. Then Cody remembered something from the night before. "Is what Diaz said true?" he asked. "Are you a traitor?"

"NO!" Derek jumped to his feet. "I never!" Derek shook his head and sat back down. He didn't say anything for a moment. Then he sighed. "I was working in Barcelona, I fell in love with this woman, things got . . . well, you know how they get with a Latin woman."

"No." Cody's eyes widened. "Tell me everything!"

Derek was about to answer then caught himself. "Every man has to learn that lesson for himself." He stood and began pacing around the room. "Anyway, turns out she was a spy for the other side. She bugged my phone, stole my computer . . . some people thought I was in on it."

"You made a mistake," Cody said. "It happens."

"I was sloppy, I'm lucky I didn't lose my job," Derek replied.

There was a knock at the door.

"Cody?" Sabeen said from the hallway.

"Hide!" Cody ordered.

Derek looked under the bed then started to run to the bathroom. The door began to open. He wasn't going to make it. Derek quickly jumped into the bed and pulled the blanket over him. Seeing the large form under the blanket, Cody knew he couldn't explain that. He quickly jumped under the blanket as well.

Sabeen walked into the room. "You're going to be late again."

Cody poked his head out from the blanket. "I'm coming," he said.

Sabeen looked confused. She raised a finger toward the form

under the covers — the form much too big to be Cody's body alone. "Um . . ."

"Thank you," Cody snapped. "Good-bye!"

Sabeen gave the bed a second look then slowly exited. Once the door shut, Derek poked his head out.

"You could land a helicopter on this bed!" he exclaimed.

Cody jumped out of bed. "Did you come up here for a particular reason?"

"Yes," replied Derek. "The director's in London. He wants to talk to you." He pulled out a cell phone, pushed a button, and then handed it to Cody. While Cody waited for the director to answer, he smiled as Derek struggled to climb out of the giant bed.

A click on the line let him know the director was there. "Yes, sir," Cody said.

"With all the dignitaries in town, the president asked me to come here personally," said the director. "You got anything for me?"

"Yes, we do," Cody replied. "Where should we meet?"

"London Eye," said the director. "In one hour."

Cody hung up the phone just as Derek finally made his way out of the bed.

"Did he ask about me?" inquired Derek.

Cody shook his head.

"He will," Derek assured him. "Derek Burnett is working his way back. And when I do, things are going to be different. Next time, *I'm* getting the big bed!"

Making sure the coast was clear, Derek quickly exited the bedroom. Cody threw on a shirt and walked to the sink. He picked up his toothbrush and toothpaste, but as he brought the open tube close to his brush, his hand began to shake. He ended up squeezing a large glob of toothpaste onto his hand instead of the brush.

Cody didn't worry about it too much. It was probably just a little muscle spasm. People had them all the time. After all, he'd been through a lot in the last few days.

Using the brush, Cody scraped some toothpaste from his hand and brought it closer to his mouth. His hand began to shake again, this time much harder. As much as he tried, he couldn't get the brush to his mouth. He set the toothpaste down, and grabbed the brush with both hands. The brush shook harder as Cody used all his might to bring it closer. Finally, his hand went crazy and brushed his cheek, nose, ears, everywhere but his mouth.

Cody set the brush down and looked at his trembling hand. It was slowly going back to normal. He glanced up at his reflection in the mirror and saw that toothpaste was smeared all over his face. With his other hand, he reached up and rubbed his jaw. There was a dull ache in the back of his mouth.

"Uh, oh."

That was the last thing Cody Banks remembered.

16

REMOTE CONTROL

Emily watched as Cody marched into the dining room. As always, he was late. Mrs. Kenworth and the other students were already seated around the long table.

"Look who finally showed up," Marcel remarked.

"Getting a little extra sleep?" Mrs. Kenworth said cheerfully. "Making sure you're well rested for the concert tonight?"

Cody moved toward his seat. "Right, that's tonight."

Emily stared at Cody. His eyes seemed a bit glazed and his movements were stiff and robotic. And when the young agent went to sit down, he missed his chair completely, landing on the floor. Emily thought he was acting a little strange — stranger than normal, anyway.

A red mail truck sat in front of the Kenworth Estate. However, this was no ordinary mail truck. Computer screens and control panels covered the truck's interior. Diaz, Kenworth, and Walther crowded around a video monitor. The monitor was tied to a hidden camera inside the Kenworth dining room. Currently, it was zoomed in on Cody Banks.

"What's he doing?" asked Diaz.

Walther held a small remote control. "He's not responding so well," he said as he carefully moved the remote control's joysticks.

"Why not?" the former agent asked.

"It takes time to calibrate the commands with each individual's brainwaves," Kenworth said calmly.

"Well, you better figure out a way to do it and fast," Diaz demanded.

Walther tapped wildly on a nearby keyboard. Another computer screen showed two sets of brainwave patterns. The wavy lines at the top of the screen represented Cody's brainwaves. They jumped sporadically as Walther quickly tried to bring them in sync with pulsing lines at the bottom of the screen, the mind control signal.

Back in the dining room, everyone laughed as Cody struggled to climb back into his seat.

"Cody's cabbaged," Sabeen said with a chuckle.

Mrs. Kenworth was appalled. "He is not!" She turned to Cody. "Are you?"

"No, of course not," Cody replied. "I'm just starving. What smells so good?"

"Beans on toast," Mrs. Kenworth replied.

"It's really good," claimed Sabeen.

"Well, um, pass the beans," said Cody.

Emily watched as Marcel handed Cody the large bowl of beans. Just before Cody set down the large bowl, his hands began to tremble. Cody smiled nervously then quickly dropped the bowl with a thud. Everyone jumped.

"Whoops," Cody joked.

When he reached for the spoon in the bowl, his hand began to tremble again. He quickly grabbed his right hand with his left and slammed it onto the table. Everyone jumped again.

This time, Cody didn't make any excuses. Instead, he reached for the spoon again with determination in his eyes. His hand grabbed the spoon, dipped out a load of beans and slowly moved them toward his plate. As it neared, his hand trembled again. It seemed to get worse, the closer it moved toward his empty plate. Finally, something snapped and Cody's hand whipped away from him, lobbing beans into Marcel's face. The young French boy was shocked.

Cody didn't seem to notice the mishap. Instead, he dipped the spoon into the bowl of beans once again. This time, the spoon began to shake immediately. When he removed it from the bowl, it shook so violently, it sprayed everyone around the table with beans.

Emily pulled a few beans from her hair and stared in disbelief as Cody went back for yet another spoonful. He seemed oblivious to the bean-covered kids around him and was determined to get a spoonful of beans onto his plate.

Now the spoon barely made it to the bowl before his hand went crazy. He flung spoonful after heaping spoonful of beans around the room.

* * *

Back in the mail truck, Diaz was panicking. "This is crazy!" he shouted. "Everyone's going to think he's insane!"

"Wait . . ." Walther said, adjusting the tiny joysticks.

Kenworth pointed to the monitor displaying Cody's brainwaves. They slowly began to match the mind control frequency on the bottom of the screen. Soon, the two patterns were identical.

"There." Walther smiled. "We are in complete control."

Back in the Kenworth dining room, Cody abruptly dropped the spoon. He stiffly dabbed at the corner of his mouth with his napkin and stood.

"Come to think of it," he said, "I'm not so hungry after all. If you'll excuse me." Cody stood, then walked out of the dining room without a second look.

Mouth open in shock, Emily looked at the other students. They all just sat there, not believing what had just happened. They were also completely covered with beans.

17

KEEPING AN EYE ON CODY

From a front window, Emily watched as Cody Banks, stepped outside. At first, he had seemed nice enough, but now she wasn't so sure. She had certainly forgiven him for bumbling into her surveillance operation, especially since he offered plenty of new information. She was even looking forward to working with him on the case. But since he disappeared the night before, and was now acting so strangely, she thought she should keep an eye on him.

Emily watched as Cody pulled out his cell phone and talked to someone. He hung up as a black cab appeared. The rear passenger door opened and Cody climbed inside.

As the cab pulled away, Emily raced outside and waved to a car she had waiting nearby. It pulled up and she hopped into the back.

"Follow that car," she told the driver.

They followed Cody to the London Eye. The Eye was a giant, four hundred and fifty foot Ferris wheel built for the Millennium Celebration in the year 2000. Emily stepped out of her car and watched as Cody bought a ticket and stepped into one of the Eye's large pods. The glass pod was almost empty except for three men facing the opposite direction, taking in the sights.

The pod doors closed and the wheel began to turn. Emily purchased a ticket herself and stepped into the adjacent pod. Several other tourists joined her, but her attention was on Cody. She pulled out a pair of binoculars and trained them on him. He merely stood there, facing the closed glass door, seeming not to notice the breathtaking view around him.

She continued to watch him as their pods made the long trip to the top then back down to the ground. Cody didn't move at all during the entire trip. When his pod returned to the platform and the doors opened, he still didn't move, in fact, neither did the tourists behind him. However, another man joined them. Emily focused her binoculars on the new arrival and recognized him immediately. It was the director of the CIA.

The director said something to Cody, but the young agent barely moved. Instead, the three tourists turned around. It was Diaz, Kenworth, and Walther. Surprised, the director shot a look to Cody then Walther sprayed some sort of mist into the man's face from a tiny silver canister. Cody merely stood there as the director fell unconscious. Once on the ground, Walther and Kenworth hunched over the director and opened his mouth.

Emily couldn't believe what she saw. She pulled out her camera phone and began snapping digital pictures of the entire scene.

18

A POP IN THE MOUTH

When Cody finally stepped off the London Eye, Emily followed him. Cody walked up to a black cab and stepped inside. Emily ran to the other side of the cab and climbed in as well.

"Uh, excuse me, Miss," Cody's handler stammered.

"Don't worry," said Emily. "I know who you really are. Drive!"

"I don't know what you are talking about," Derek said, worried about blowing his cover.

"I'm an undercover agent with British Intelligence," said Emily.

"You too?" Derek asked in amazement. "No wonder the malls are empty. They got all the kids!"

"She's lying, Derek," snapped Cody.

She turned to Derek. "We don't have much time. Kenworth and Diaz implanted Cody with the mind-control device and he led them to the director."

"What?" asked Cody, acting very surprised. "That's crazy!"

Emily held up her phone with a crystal clear image of Cody, the director, Diaz, and Kenworth.

Derek stared at the cell phone. "I don't believe it."

"I took this twenty minutes ago," Emily reported.

"No, I mean, where did you get this phone?" asked Derek.

"Standard Agency issue," Emily replied.

"'Standard?!" Derek exclaimed. "When this is over I'm getting all new stuff!"

"DRIVE!" Emily shouted.

Derek hit the gas and peeled away from the curb. He hit a button on the dash and all the doors locked.

"Stop the car, Derek," Cody ordered.

"I knew something was going on," said Derek.

"We've got to get it out of him," said Emily.

"How?" asked Derek.

"I don't know," Emily replied. "I guess we have to find a way to . . ."

Cody reached over the backseat, making a grab for Derek. Derek slammed his elbow into Cody's forehead. The young agent slumped back in his seat.

". . . knock him out," Emily finished.

Derek parked the cab in an alley then joined Emily and Cody in the backseat. She propped up the young agent and peered into his mouth. She saw a tiny silver object embedded in one of Cody's molars.

"There it is," said Emily. "Do you have a hammer?"

"You're going to take a hammer to the boy's mouth?" Derek asked in surprise. "Remind me not to take a nap around you."

"Okay, we'll make some calls and find a dentist," said Emily.

"There's no time," Derek said, reaching into Cody's pocket. He pulled out the long tube of breath mints.

Emily's eyes widened. "You pick now to steal his candy?"

"It's not candy," Derek said as he popped a mint into his mouth. Then he turned and spit it out the open window. The tiny mint exploded in midair. "It's an explosive."

"You're going to kill him," Emily cried.

"Not if I use the right amount." Derek began to break apart another mint in his hand. "Let me see, 20 grains equals . . ."

"Do you know what you're doing?" Emily asked.

". . . one scruple," Derek continued, counting to himself, still chipping away at the piece of candy. "Three scruples equal . . ."

"Derek!" said Emily.

"Never interrupt a man when he's trying to break down the apothecaries' table," said Derek. "One dram, three grains . . ."

Derek chipped an even smaller piece away and crammed it against Cody's back tooth. He quickly closed his mouth.

Emily turned her head. "I can't look."

She heard a small pop then looked back at Cody. Waking up slowly, he opened his mouth to speak and small drifts of smoke flowed out. Suddenly he was wide-awake.

"OW!!!" Cody yelled.

Emily turned to Derek. "How'd you know how to do that?"

"Just cause I went to community college," Derek said proudly, "doesn't mean I'm not a brilliant man."

Cody groaned and rubbed his forehead.

"Why does my head hurt so much?" asked Cody.

"Uh, you fell," Derek said nervously.

"What happened?" Cody asked. "I don't remember anything after brushing my teeth."

"They implanted you with the mind-control device," Emily told him.

"And now they've got the director," Derek added.

"The director?" asked Cody. "Why?"

"I don't know what they can possibly hope to pull," Derek said. Then his face lit up. "The Gala, tonight! Twelve leaders from twelve countries all in the same place!"

"If they get all twelve under their control," Cody said, "they could do anything!" He reached for his phone. "I'll call for backup."

"I don't think so." Derek put a hand on his phone. "They've got the director of the CIA under their control and we're the only ones who know about it." He turned to Emily. "What would you do if you were them?"

"Convince both our governments that we were dirty," Emily answered.

Derek shook his head. "There's a bounty on our heads for sure."

"But we can't fight them on our own," said Emily. "If we're going to stop them we're going to need help, highly trained operatives that the director can't turn against us. People we can trust."

Cody Banks smiled. "No problem."

19

A LITTLE HELP FROM YOUR FRIENDS

At Heathrow airport, Cody, Emily, and Derek waited outside the terminal for the Concorde, the fastest passenger jet in the world. When it landed, Cody smiled as his friends from Kamp Woody stepped through the gate. Bender appeared first, followed by Ryan, and then Marisa and the rest of the "ninja girls." The group of young agents looked ready for action as they strode through the airport.

Emily looked at Cody in disbelief. "You chartered the Concorde?"

"How did you pay for it?" asked Derek.

Cody held up his father's credit card. "I'd say this qualifies as an emergency."

That night, Buckingham Palace was lit like a Christmas tree for the evening's grand event. Foreign dignitaries and honored guests from all over the world arrived in limousines and came dressed in the finest tuxedos and evening gowns.

Cody Banks, sporting a tuxedo himself, hid in the shadows as the bus from the Hastings Academy of Music approached. He watched as Neville, Derek's accomplice, waved the bus to a stop. The door opened and Maestro Hans Jerkovitch stepped out.

"I am here with my orchestra," said the maestro. "Is there a problem?"

"Not at all," Neville lied, his ill-fitting security guard's uniform sagged a bit. "We've arranged special parking for you across the way there." He pointed to an open garage. Kumar, also wearing a security uniform waved them over with a flashlight.

"How kind," Hans said as he stepped back into the bus.

"Just doing my bit, sir," Neville replied.

The bus followed Neville's instructions and pulled into the garage. Once it was inside, Neville and Kumar slammed the garage door shut and slapped a large padlock onto the door.

That's one orchestra that won't be performing tonight, Cody thought.

Once inside and backstage, Cody peeked through the closed curtains. Large sparkling chandeliers shone over the grand ballroom. The walls were covered with priceless art and the floor with well-dressed guests seated at tables.

He scanned the audience and spotted a number of important leaders from various nations. Unfortunately, several of them also showed signs of already being under mind control. The Egyptian president's hand shook as he took a sip of tea and the German prime minister displayed an unusual facial tick.

Then Cody spotted the director of the CIA alongside the president of the United States. Cody didn't know if they had gotten to the president, but unfortunately, he knew for sure that they had gotten to the director.

Cody glanced back at his fellow "musicians." He, Emily, and the agents from Kamp Woody were all formally dressed and carried musical instruments. They would be taking the place of the Hastings orchestra that evening.

Jo Kenworth stood on the stage, finishing her speech. "So, my loving husband and I decided what better way to celebrate the children than to showcase their talents by sponsoring an international youth orchestra," she said proudly. "One child was chosen from each country represented here today."

Backstage, a nervous stocky man approached the group of young agents.

"You were late," he said. "It's not done. I tell you it's not done." He eyed the group. "Wait a minute, where's your conductor? Where's Maestro Jerkovitch?"

"Um, he'll be here any second," Cody replied quickly.

"Lords and Ladies," Mrs. Kenworth announced, "esteemed guests, Prime Minister, Your Majesty." She bowed toward the queen. "The Hastings School of Music presents, your International Youth Orchestra led by guest conductor, Maestro Hans Jerkovitch."

The guests applauded and the curtain opened. Cody and the others walked onto the stage and took their seats.

Mrs. Kenworth took a seat beside Dr. Kenworth. When she looked back at the stage, she did a double take at the young orchestra. It was clear she knew something was wrong. "Wait a minute . . ."

Then it was Cody's turn to be surprised as Derek walked onto the stage. Dressed in a tuxedo as well, he waved to the crowd then approached the podium.

"We were preparing to play Hayden's Fifth for you tonight," Derek told the audience in a thick German accent. "But I said to the kids, 'He was a hack, why waste your time?'"

The members of the audience looked around in disbelief. Jo Kenworth was about to stand, but Dr. Kenworth grabbed her arm and pulled her back to her seat. He leaned back and motioned to a group of security guards. The guards slowly walked toward the stage.

"Instead I say to the young people of today, write your own song," Derek continued. "A song that will make the whole world sing, a song of love and special things. So inspired by the coming together of all peoples," Derek added, "this is their song to you."

Derek turned to the kids and raised his baton. They readied their instruments. When Maestro Derek signaled them to begin, the children played . . . horribly. Years of blow-off band classes and uninspired music lessons clashed as the group of inexperienced musicians tried to play together for the first time.

It's a good thing the CIA doesn't want these kids for their music abilities, Cody thought.

The audience looked at each other in disbelief. Was this some sort of joke? The security guards moved closer but not too close. Even as bad as the performance was, it seemed as if they wouldn't disrupt it in front of the dignified audience.

When they finished playing, the audience members gave them polite, yet undeserved, applause.

Derek leaned toward the kids. "Bow and let's get out of here."

The kids began to leave when the ambassador from India stood.

"Pardon me, please," said the ambassador. "I have been truly moved by the events of this week and by the beautiful music represented here tonight." The rest of the audience gave him a confused look. Undaunted, the man continued. "I hereby pledge the government of India will give twenty million dollars to benefit the Children's Rights Organization!" He gave a nod to his aide who began to make a call on a cell phone.

The audience exchanged their looks of confusion to those of delight as they erupted into applause.

The Egyptian president stood as well. "Egypt joins its brothers and pledges *thirty* million dollars."

The audience applauded louder.

Cody couldn't believe it. One by one, the other great leaders stood and made similar pledges.

The German prime minister stood as well. "It is truly historic, what has happened here today," he announced. "I can think of no better man, no one who cares more about the needs of children than Dr. Duncan Kenworth."

Dr. Kenworth stood and waved to the applauding crowd.

The prime minister continued. “I nominate him to be trustee of this money, and to spend it generously as he sees fit.”

The doctor acted surprised. “Me? No, surely . . .”

The applause grew louder.

So this was their plan, Cody thought. Diaz and Kenworth weren’t trying to take over the nations’ leaders for power. They were doing it for money.

The security guards placed their hands to their ears. Someone must have given them instructions to move in on the orchestra while the crowd was focused on Kenworth and the world leaders.

Cody turned to Ryan. “We’re going to need a distraction.”

Ryan reached into a bag and pulled out two large ferrets. “Will these do?”

20

JUST DESSERTS

An older refined woman sat at her table, admiring her dessert. She held the plate in front of her face, admiring the huge mounds of sorbet and finely crafted spun sugar. It looked as tasty as it did artful.

She moved the dish toward the table and looked up only to see one of Ryan's ferrets standing on the table in front of her. Baring its teeth, it hissed at her and the woman flung her dessert over her shoulder. She ran screaming from the table.

At another table, the other ferret climbed up a mink stole on a woman's back. The man seated next to her stroked the stole until he realized it was alive. He screamed. The wearer of the stole screamed. Then their entire table screamed.

Cody watched as all of the distinguished guests began to panic. Some of them tried to catch the elusive ferrets while others simply ran from the ballroom. The dignitaries' private security guards raced in and ushered them away. Meanwhile, Kenworth's security guards shoved through the panic-stricken crowd toward the stage.

"Bender, make a hole," Cody ordered.

Bender baled from the stage, roared in defiance, and then plowed through the four security guards closest to them. Then the "ninja girls" jumped and flipped from the stage and took on a few more guards. The underpaid, overweight security guards were no match for their martial arts training.

Dr. Kenworth madly pushed his way toward the exit. Cody leapt from the stage then looked back at Derek and Emily.

"Go!" Derek yelled. "We'll catch up!"

Once outside the palace, Cody followed Kenworth as he ran to the red mail truck parked suspiciously out front. The doctor flung open the back door and jumped inside.

When Cody reached the van, he didn't swing open the door immediately. Instead, he carefully cracked the door open and peeked inside. Walther sat in front of a large computer monitor. The doctor leaned over him.

"Where's Diaz?" asked Kenworth.

"I thought he was with you," Walther replied.

"Who cares!" Kenworth barked. "Move over!" The doctor shoved Walther out of the chair and sat down in front of one of the monitors.

"Should be coming up any second now," Walther said.

They watched the screen as numbers slowly rose into view. However, these weren't ordinary numbers. They were dollar amounts matching the pledges the dignitaries made earlier. First twenty million, then thirty million, then forty million — the numbers slowly rose until the total reached four hundred and fifty million dollars. Kenworth and Walther seemed very pleased.

Cody swung open the door. "Too bad you'll never get to spend that money."

"What money?" Kenworth laughed. "It's in a blind account in a bank in Bermuda. Even if you can prove I've done anything, you'll never touch the money. It's untraceable!"

Staring at the computer screen, Walther tapped Kenworth on the shoulder. "Uh, sir?"

The doctor turned just in time to see the total amount of money drop from 450 million to 420, to 380, and below.

"Do something!" Kenworth yelled.

Walther pushed past Kenworth and began typing. "I'm trying."

Cody laughed. "I think you just got double-crossed."

"DIAZ!!!" Kenworth roared.

"It looks like you're broke," said Cody.

Suddenly, the police surrounded the mail truck.

"And going to jail," Cody added.

"NOOO!!!" Kenworth cried.

Cody backed away as the police arrested Dr. Kenworth and Walther. Obviously, Victor Diaz had double-crossed Kenworth and stolen the money from his bank account. "But to hack into a secured bank file," Cody said, thinking aloud, "there's no way he could have done it so fast, unless . . ."

Cody looked up and saw the headquarters of the World European Bank. The skyscraper pierced the dark sky with its rows of satellite dishes on the roof.

". . . he was in the bank itself and tapped into the mainframe!"

21

SOMETIMES, THE CHEESE GETS THE MOUSE

Cody carefully stepped over the unconscious security guards and quietly made his way down the dark hallway. A faint light shone from the open door at the end. He also heard typing on a keyboard and whistling. It had to be Diaz.

As the young agent cautiously approached the open door, the typing stopped. Cody froze as hard footsteps grew louder. Diaz stepped out of the door then froze himself when he saw Cody Banks.

"You didn't really think you were going to get away with it?" Cody asked.

Diaz chuckled as he stepped closer. "You don't give up do you? No, matter how hopeless, no matter how misguided your judgment, something in you just won't let go." Showing no fear, he moved even closer. "I was just like you once."

"I'm nothing like you!" Cody yelled.

He sprung at the former agent, sending a flying kick toward his chest. Diaz blocked the kick and Cody followed with several quick punches. Having taught Cody the moves in the first place, his former instructor easily countered them all.

Then Diaz took the offensive. With precision timing, he swung and kicked at the young agent. But Cody had been a good student. He easily evaded Diaz's blows and countered with a few of his own.

Diaz jumped, spun, and caught the young agent off guard. He landed a kick, knocking Cody into the wall. Then Diaz smashed the glass on a nearby firebox and removed the ax inside. He swung it madly at Cody who barely ducked out of the way. Diaz backed Cody up against the elevator and slashed again. Cody dove out of the way as the axe chopped into the elevator's control panel. It sizzled, sparked, and opened the elevator doors, exposing the open shaft.

Cody ran to one of the fallen guards and retrieved his nightstick. He spun it around with a flourish, showing he was skilled with that particular weapon.

Diaz hacked and chopped at Cody with the axe, but the young agent managed to deflect the blows with a mere swat of the stick. Cody felt confident with the new weapon. Then he realized his former instructor's strategy. Diaz wasn't actually trying to hit him; he was merely maneuvering Cody back to the open elevator shaft.

Unfortunately, Cody's realization came too late. With his final block of the axe, Diaz chopped Cody's nightstick in half and slammed his boot against Cody's chest. Cody fell back and tumbled down the elevator shaft.

Diaz laughed and dropped the axe. He pushed through the stairwell door and headed upstairs.

In the elevator shaft, Cody Banks appeared to rise in midair. When he stood level with the floor, he hopped out of the shaft. The elevator he stood on continued to rise. Derek and Emily stood inside.

"We thought maybe you could use some help," said Derek.

Cody smiled. "Great timing."

"Cody," Derek grabbed his arm. "Before Diaz left he took everything," Derek reported. "He has everything he needs to mass produce the mind-control device."

"If he gets away he could do anything," Emily added. "Start wars, overthrow governments, there'll be no stopping him."

There was a low rumble coming from above. "He's on the roof," Cody said confidently.

"Why would he . . ." said Emily.

"Helicopter!" Cody exclaimed as he slammed open the stairwell door.

Cody ran up the stairs and blew through the door leading to the roof. He stepped out to see a helicopter warming up. Its rotors turning faster and faster. Diaz sat at the controls.

Derek and Emily stepped out behind him. "Great, how are we supposed to bring down a helicopter?" asked Derek. "We need a bazooka or something."

Cody looked around and saw some welding equipment. He pointed to one of the tanks. "You throw one of those tanks up into the blades and what'll happen?" asked Cody.

Derek smiled. "We'd have our bazooka."

"But they're so heavy," said Emily. "How can we get him to fly right over us?"

Cody thought fast. "It's not hard," he said. "All it takes is a little cheese." He ran toward the helicopter. "Be ready!"

Cody sprinted out onto the roof just as the helicopter lifted off. When he was twenty feet away, he stopped.

Diaz scowled at him from the cockpit. He pushed on the stick and the helicopter tilted forward. The helicopter moved toward Cody Banks, the rotors aiming right for his head.

Cody waited for the approaching helicopter as long as he dared. "Come on," he whispered. "Closer . . . closer."

Then Cody took off running. With Diaz close behind, he ran toward Derek and Emily. He saw that they had one of the tanks upside down and leaning against the welder's cart. Derek held a large wrench in one hand and the tank was aimed at the helicopter.

"That's right, come on over," Derek taunted. "We got something for you!"

Cody ran faster, but the helicopter flew closer. He could feel the wind from the rotors on the back of his neck.

As he approached the side of the building, Cody turned to Derek. "Now!" he yelled.

Derek slammed the wrench onto the tank's valve. It broke away and a column of gas shot out one end. The force launched the tank toward the helicopter's rotors.

Even with the tank launched, the rotors still gained on Cody. He quickly approached the edge of the building. He had nowhere to go.

Cody leapt over the edge.

"CODY!" Emily cried.

The tank collided with the helicopter's rotors and exploded.

The building shook as a chain reaction began, exploding the helicopter's fuel tank. The former agent's helicopter blew up in a ball of fire that lit the London skyline.

As Cody hung off of one of the building's many satellite dishes, he watched as bits of burning metal fell past him to the street below.

"Hey," Cody yelled. "Somebody want to throw me a rope?"

22

SIR CODY BANKS?

Cody knelt between Emily and Derek. They were all dressed in their finest agency suits. Before them, stood an older woman with a sword. They weren't in any danger, however. Instead, they were being knighted by the queen of England.

The queen lightly tapped each of Cody's shoulders with the sword. "Rise," she said, "*Sir* Cody Banks."

The three stood as they were presented to the small group in attendance. The director of the CIA and Cody's friends from Kamp Woody clapped loudly. Kumar even wiped a tear from one eye.

Cody felt very proud, not only for himself, but also for Emily, a girl who turned out to be a topnotch secret agent. And for Derek as well. Cody didn't think Derek was much of an agent at first, but his handler soon proved he was more than the washed-up spy others thought he was.

Cody knew that no one but the few agents and officials present could know about his knighthood or the heroic acts that earned it. To the rest of the world, he was just a kid, not a great junior agent for the CIA. Cody wondered if it was time he started being a better kid instead.

The director walked up and shook their hands. He stopped when he got to Cody Banks. "You know," the director said, "we've got a situation brewing in the South Seas that's going to need some looking into."

Derek nudged Cody's arm. "What do you say, Cody?"

Cody paused for a moment. The thought of another adventure did appeal to him on some level. Then again, he thought back to what Emily had told him, about how being an agent isn't his life; it was just his job. And maybe it *was* time for a vacation.

"If it's okay with you, sir," Cody said. "I thought I'd go home for awhile. Basketball tryouts are next week. I was thinking about getting a job at the mall, going to the prom, a few things like that."

The director smiled. "You mean you want to have a normal life, Agent Banks?"

"For as long as I can, sir," Cody replied.

Emily and Derek smiled at each other. Derek put his arm around Cody and rubbed his head.

"Well you're not completely off the hook," the director added. "I think your father has a mission for you."

23

THE NEW MISSION

In the hot sun, on his hands and knees, Agent Cody Banks, junior member of the CIA, pulled weeds in the backyard. Cody smiled as he wiped a gloved hand across his sweaty brow. It was hard work, but it was much more than that. It was one of his family chores. It was part of being a kid.

"You missed one," Alex said as he casually walked by.

Thinking fast, Cody dove for the nearby garden hose. He aimed the nozzle at his annoying little brother and fired. Alex squealed as the cool stream of water drenched him. The young boy reached down, grabbed a handful of mud and returned fire. Cody was laughing so hard, he didn't duck in time and a glob of mud splattered onto his face. Cody dropped the hose and countered with his own handful of mud.

This was what being a kid was all about. Having fun, acting stupid, and not having to worry about international espionage for a while. Right at that moment, Cody didn't have a care in the world. It was great to be a kid again.

Cody's father stepped onto the back porch with a handful of mail. He was about to sit down when he peered closer at the open credit card statement in his hand.

"Forty-five thousand dollars!" his dad cried.

"Uh, oh." Cody froze.

"You chartered the Concorde?" Mr. Banks asked in amazement. His stare darted from the credit card statement to his oldest, mud-covered, son.

Cody dropped a handful of mud and sprinted through the back gate.

"CODY!!!" his father yelled as he gave chase.